Handful of Peaches

Peaches Monroe's Diary

BOOK #1 of 4

ANGIE PEPPER

Chapter 1

Before I became internationally famous as a curvy underwear model, I was just a girl working at a bookstore.

One Saturday, I was standing on a wooden stool, trying to solve a major problem. A sweet aroma from the building next door, Donut Joe's, kept wafting in through the air vent. I couldn't take the temptation for another minute.

I was blocking the vent with packing tape when the front door opened. A guy came running into the bookstore, breathing heavily. A gorgeous young dark-haired guy.

He didn't see me standing on the stool. He slammed into me with his gorgeous body. I toppled off and fell right into his arms.

The handsome stranger didn't just catch me. He held me. He held me like I belonged to him.

I stared up into his gorgeous green eyes. Was I dreaming? The light from the window made his dark-brown hair glow like a halo.

Then he opened his mouth and said the most captivating thing: "What kind of an idiot stands on a stool when there's a perfectly good ladder available?"

"Ladders are overrated. And it's good to challenge yourself."

He grinned, still holding me in his strong arms. "You're quick at justifying your bad life choices, aren't you?"

"You have no idea."

"I can't really judge you," he said. "I've made some pretty questionable life choices myself."

"Such as running into stores like a charging rhinoceros and knocking girls off chairs?"

"For a start."

He continued to cradle me tenderly, like I was a lost kitten who'd fallen from a tree, and not a curvy twenty-two-year-old in a bridesmaid dress.

The smell of his skin reached my nose. Oh, mercy. He smelled better than the wicked donuts from next door.

"You can set me down anywhere," I said. "My employee is due in at any moment, and it will ruin my authority as the store manager for him to see me like this."

"I'll set you down, but first you have to make me a promise. No more standing on chairs."

"I'll use the ladder next time."

"There's my girl." He set me down gently.

The man looked so familiar, from his square jaw to his dazzling green eyes. Where did I know him from?

He glanced over his shoulder at the window then asked, "Do you have somewhere I can hide out for a few minutes?"

"We have a washroom, but it's for customers only."

He went to the New Arrivals table and grabbed a book at random.

"I'm a customer," he said. "I'm buying this."

It was a book for ladies with bladder control issues.

"Excellent choice," I said with a straight face. "The washroom's at the back, through the bead curtain. The light switch is in the last place you'd expect it to be."

He raised one sexy dark eyebrow. "Should I take a flashlight?"

"Just grope around in the dark until you get lucky."

He raised his eyebrow even higher. "It's been a while since a beautiful girl has said that to me."

I resisted the urge to melt into a puddle of giggles. I just smiled, playing it cool.

He glanced over to the front windows. A throng of people were approaching the store.

"I'm trying to shake someone who's pure evil," he explained. "If anyone asks, I'm not here." He held my eyes with his hypnotic gaze. "We can trust each other," he said confidently.

"We can?"

There was a ruckus outside the front door. People were running back and forth. A big guy whizzed by with a camera.

The front door opened, and suddenly a whole TV news crew came rushing into Bookworm Books.

At the front was a woman with bright-red hair and heavy makeup. She gave me a disappointed look.

"You're just some boring girl," she said, right to my face.

I checked over my shoulder. My handsome hero had disappeared.

I turned back to the nasty redhead.

"Can this boring girl help you with anything?" I asked sweetly. "Maybe a self-help book about how not to be such a giant—"

The woman cut me off, asking her crew, "He wouldn't have run in here, would he? I doubt he's ever read a book."

The cameraman chuckled. "Meat puppets like him can barely read their cue cards."

A guy lugging other equipment said to the cameraman, "You're just jealous because you're not a pretty boy with fainting fans."

The redhead broke from the pack and strolled around Bookworm Books, her upper lip curled up in disgust. "I thought all the little bookstores shut down," she said.

Even though I knew not to argue with people of low intelligence, I said, "You're standing inside a bookstore now, so unless this is a dream, we can deduce that not all of the bookstores are closed."

She snorted, as if I were the stupid one, not her.

I continued patiently, "You see, we have all these shelves full of books because this *is* a bookstore."

The woman wrinkled her nose and sniffed the air contemptuously. "Thanks for nothing. Good luck with the books."

"Good luck with your attitude."

She sneered as she looked me over. "Good luck with whatever that dress is supposed to be."

What did she mean by that? My curves were rocking in that dress. Was I going to have to punch her in the neck? She wasn't a customer, so technically, neck-punching wasn't against store policy.

Before I could get my hands on her, the crew and the woman left as quickly as they'd come. The front door closed with a cheerful jingle of the bells, and it was just me again. Just me and the sweet vanilla aroma coming in through the vent from Donut Joe's.

The door to the customer washroom opened and closed. My handsome hero came walking up, weaving his way around tall shelves crammed with books.

I held my hand to my chest, the fabric of my bridesmaid dress crinkly. "You scared me."

His voice was even deeper and sexier now. "Did you already forget about me?"

"I thought you left out the back door. Plus I was distracted by Lady Satan, with her film crew."

He held up the book he'd taken with him to the washroom. "This is very informative. What do I owe you?"

I started doing busywork at the store's counter, stacking the Post-It notepads, putting away the stamp, and straightening the pens.

"You don't have to buy that book," I said. "Men don't even have kegel muscles."

"They don't? That's not fair."

I stared up at his beautiful green eyes. They crinkled at the sides when he smiled. My own eyes were blue, and they disappeared more than they crinkled. I'd inherited blond hair and blue eyes from my mother, plus more curves than were fashionable. My handsome hero was a generous man, flirting with a chubby girl like me.

Casually, I asked, "So, are you a criminal, or a celebrity?"

"Depends on who you ask."

"You look familiar."

"So do you." His gaze traveled down my body.

I tried to suck in my tummy. I was already strapped into two pairs of tummy-flatteners. My organs had nowhere left to go.

With a sexy growl to his voice, he asked, "Do you always dress so fancy at work?"

"I'm going to a wedding any minute now."

"A wedding." He took two steps back and gave me an appraising look, his arms crossed.

He looked dressy himself, in sharply creased gray trousers and a button-down shirt, rolled up at the cuffs to reveal muscular arms with a smattering of dark hairs. Even his forearms looked familiar, like I'd already spent countless hours staring at them.

My eyes were starting to hurt from staring at him. I'd forgotten how to blink.

He said, "It's a shame you're getting married. Just my luck."

"I'm not getting married. I'm just a bridesmaid. My cousin Tina's getting married today."

"Ah." He nodded. "And this is all happening shortly? Why are you here, in this charming bookstore?"

"I'm waiting for my employee to arrive, and then I'll call for a ride."

"My driver's nearby. I could give you a lift, as a thank-you for helping me hide from Lady Satan."

I wasn't comfortable taking him up on his offer, so I didn't respond, except to say, "That reporter was nasty. I don't blame you for hiding."

"What's your name?"

"Petra Monroe," I said. "Everyone calls me Peaches. Peaches Monroe."

"That's the perfect name for you. Because you're sweet as a peach, aren't you?"

I batted my eyelashes. "I can be sweet."

He held out his hand. "I'm Dalton Deangelo."

I laughed. "Yeah, right! You're Dalton Deangelo, the actor I watch every week in my favorite show, *One Vamp to Love*."

"I am."

I stopped laughing. "You are." I swore under my breath. "You're Drake Cheshire, two hundred years old and forever young. You look so different without the pale makeup."

"You're familiar with my work."

"Slightly," I said. "You seem different in person. You're not... shirtless and emotional."

"I can be shirtless and emotional if that's what you need." He reached for the hem of his shirt and tugged it up playfully.

"Stop! I'm a mere mortal. My head would explode, and I need my head for my bridesmaid duties. Tina would be so mad if I showed up for her wedding with no head, so don't you dare, Drake Cheshire."

"Ordinarily, I don't like people calling me by my character name, but it's cute when you say it, Peaches." He picked up some miniature journals we kept by the computer and flipped through them. "Are you meeting your date at the wedding?"

"I don't have a date."

"No boyfriend? Or girlfriend?"

"Neither."

He pouted playfully. "Nobody likes going to a wedding alone. How about I arrange a date for you?"

"Oh, Mr. Deangelo, I couldn't ask you to do that. You probably have a very busy life and lots of things to do."

He raised his eyebrows, looking more like devious Drake by the minute. "Me? Oh, no. I was going to send my butler."

I crossed my arms. "Your butler?"

"If he's not good enough, then how about me?"

The door jingled open. My sixteen-year-old employee, Garnet, came running in, apologizing for being late. Without looking at Dalton, he ran around the counter and tossed his book bag next to my purse.

"Get going," Garnet said. His dark hair was messier than usual. "I slept in, and—"

Garnet looked up at Dalton Deangelo.

Dalton gave him a Drake Cheshire grin.

Garnet raised his hand and pointed at the handsome actor. "You!"

"Me," Dalton said.

"You!" Garnet jabbed his finger at the man. "You!"

"I've seen this before," the actor said to me. To Garnet, he said, "It's me, all right. Would you like an autograph?"

Garnet frowned and folded his arms. "No." He looked at me and asked, "Is this really happening? Is he actually here, in our bookstore?"

"Not for long," Dalton said. "I'm taking Peaches to her cousin's wedding. I trust you'll be able to manage the store without her?"

Garnet gave me a quizzical look. "Do you two know each other?"

"We're friends," Dalton said.

At the exact same time, I contradicted him by saying, "We just met."

Dalton explained to Garnet, "I make friends quickly."

Garnet snorted and said to me, "He's very pushy. These Hollywood types always get what they want."

I put my arm around Garnet and explained to Dalton, "Young Garnet here is going through a tough-guy phase. I'm sure that as soon as you leave, he'll regret not getting a picture with you."

Garnet's shoulders stiffened under my arm. He narrowed his eyes at Dalton.

Dalton tilted his head. "How old are you, young man?"

"None of your business," Garnet said.

"He's sixteen," I said. "And I'm twenty-two. But, unlike young Garnet, I'm past the jaded stage."

Garnet ducked out from under my arm and busied himself looking through the custom order pile.

Dalton's expression remained calm and friendly. He seemed unperturbed by Garnet's rudeness. I guessed he was used to all sorts of different reactions from regular folks like us. I was a little surprised Garnet was being such a grump. He had a famous singer for a mother and another one for a grandmother. I would have expected him to be more polite, or at least not hostile.

Dalton said, smoothly, "So, are we going to hit this wedding of yours, or what?"

"I'm ready to go."

"Good." He offered me his elbow.

I hesitated.

They say if you ever meet your idols, you should walk away before you're disappointed. They also say that if you meet the Buddha, you should kill him. (I don't understand that one at all.)

"This is weird," I said, not taking his elbow just yet.

"Good weird or bad weird?"

"I feel like I know you, and going somewhere with you is something I do all the time, but usually there's a plane of glass between us."

"I'm glad you're a fan of my show."

"It's the best show on TV, but I hate the cliffhangers."

His green eyes twinkled. "You *love* the cliffhangers."

"I love Drake Cheshire."

"I get that a lot."

"I bet you do."

"Peaches, you do know I'm a real person, right? I'm not an ancient vampire with a bunch of gypsy curses on me. I'm just a guy."

"Of course I know that. I'm not *completely* crazy."

Garnet snorted.

I shot the kid a warning look.

Dalton asked Garnet, "How crazy is your boss?"

"You'll see," Garnet said.

I said to the kid, "Be nicer or I'll cut your hours."

Garnet scowled and said, "Have fun at the wedding, you two."

Dalton moved toward the door. I stayed where I was, under the vent that was still pumping out donut smells.

I stared at the store's counter and felt vaguely homesick, as I always did when I had to leave before closing.

Garnet was standing in my favorite comfortable spot behind the counter, an arm's reach from the vintage yellow phone. Behind him were piles of special-order books with customer tags sticking out like multicolored paper tongues. Beyond that were all our beautiful shelves, set far enough apart that customers could walk past each other without bumping, yet close enough to encourage friendly conversation.

The bookstore was my whole life. Sometimes, in the evening, after we were closed, I'd stay behind and just hang out there in the dark, watching the traffic on Baker Street.

Dalton pulled open the front door, and the sounds of the outside world came in.

It was time for me to leave my comfort zone.

Chapter 2

Dalton and I arrived on the late side, which would have been unforgivable if I'd had any actual duties as bridesmaid, but I was simply a spare who'd been added at the last minute to balance out an extra groomsman.

I stood in my place, holding my flowers and performing my sacred duty. As the sole chubby bridesmaid, I would make everyone else look slimmer by comparison for the photos.

The wedding was for my older cousin, Tina Gardenia. She was getting married to the very hunky Luca Lowell.

My date sat patiently on his own, in the back row, through the whole ceremony.

Nobody screamed or fainted, or even recognized him. He definitely would have stolen attention away from the good-looking couple if more of the people in attendance had been avid watchers of vampire soap operas.

Because there'd been no time to introduce Dalton to my family upon arrival, the awkwardness with my parents was a treat to still look forward to.

The weather was hot for May, and the little chapel grew muggy with all the people inside.

After the ceremony, I found Dalton, and we ducked outside to the front steps as soon as we could.

"That was a beautiful ceremony," Dalton said. "Everything happened so fast. I've never been to a real wedding before."

"You only go to fake weddings?"

"Yes."

I smacked my forehead. "Oh, for the show. That's right. There have been…" I counted in my head. "Four weddings."

He looked at me as if seeing me without any clothes on.

For the record, I did not hate this feeling.

"You're a true fan of the show," he said.

"Don't let it go to your head, but yes, I have worshiped you for years."

He raised his eyebrows, looking sexy in the way only an immortal TV vampire could.

I gave him a serious look. "I said don't let it go to your head, mister. I can stop watching any time I want."

"Our ratings say otherwise."

Our conversation was interrupted by my family— my mom, dad, and Elliot—walking up.

My father dove right in, asking, "What ratings?" He squinted to protect his pale-blue eyes from the bright sun. My father had red hair, which glowed like fire in the bright sun.

Before we could answer my father's question about the ratings, my dad jumped onto a new topic. He pointed at the church and said, "What they ought to have on the ceiling is a chain of fans. You could set them up in tandem and create a stream of air."

I swung one of my fists in a supportive gesture. "You should march right in there and tell them, Dad."

He ducked his head back, forming double chins. The prospect of him actually telling someone something they ought to know, such as the optimal way to ventilate a building, was preposterous.

My mother couldn't take her eyes off my surprise date. She wore a blue dress that matched her eyes, tied with a red belt that matched her red shoes. Her toes pointed demurely together as she gazed up at Dalton.

"Peachy, who's this young man?" Most of my friends called me Peaches, but my mother called me Petra or Peachy.

I introduced everyone by their first names.

The youngest Monroe tilted his head up in that cute way only a seven-year-old could and asked, "Are you Peepee's boyfriend?"

My mother called me Peachy, but little Elliot called me Peepee. Not my favorite nickname.

Dalton did a double-take. "Peepee? I don't know anyone by that name, young man."

"Elliot!" I gave him a dirty look. "Don't call me that, you little turd monkey."

Dalton said, "You could say I'm a future old friend of Peepee's." He knelt down and shook Elliot's hand.

"You're taller than my dad," Elliot said. "Can I sit on your shoulders? I want to see everything."

Dalton leaned forward like a trained circus horse and let Elliot climb on top of his shoulders.

My mother caught my eye and loudly whispered, "He's so handsome, Peachy."

Dalton took off and ran up and down the chapel steps with Elliot squealing on his shoulders.

"Is he?" I gave a casual shrug. "I hadn't noticed, Mom. I'm not shallow like you, marrying Dad for his good looks."

At this, my father beamed.

I felt a wave of gratitude for all my riches. My family was not perfect. We had our fights and our secrets, but most of us genuinely *liked* each other, and that was just as important as love.

My mother asked, "Is he sticking around for the reception?"

I answered, "For what I'm paying him by the hour, I sure hope so."

My father shook his head. "What? You're paying that man by the hour?"

"Yes, Dad. I hired a male escort as my wedding date."

My father frowned at my mother. "Is she serious? I can't tell."

My mother said, "Peachy can't afford a male escort."

I gave her a surprised look. "How would you know?"

"You work at a bookstore," she said. "We're very proud of you, but it's not exactly a long-term career choice, I hope."

My father, his gaze on Dalton and Elliot, said, "That young man would go for top dollar, I'd imagine."

"Top dollar," my mother agreed.

"He's not an escort," I said. "He's an actor."

My mother squeezed my arm. "How clever of you, Peachy. I'm sure starving actors are available much cheaper than genuine escorts."

My father asked, "How much? I'd like to take a fellow like that up to the Cedars when my rich friends are showing off. Then I'll have something to show off, too. My new friend... What did you say his name was?"

"Dalton Deangelo," I said.

"That's funny," my mother said. "That's the name of that fellow who plays the vampire on..." Her eyes widened, and her face went pale.

My father, oblivious to my mother's reaction, asked, "How much is his hourly rate? Does he offer a discount for a half day?"

"I'm not paying him," I said.

"Is it a freebie? A sample to see if you like what you get?"

I glanced over at Dalton, who was tirelessly carrying Elliot through a maze of low shrubs.

"Something like that," I said.

Chapter 3

Dalton Deangelo gave me a look of disbelief. "You told your parents I was your paid escort?"

We were sitting in the back seat of his fancy car. His driver was taking us over to the country club where the rest of Tina and Luca's celebration would be happening.

"Not exactly," I said. "I told them you were an actor, not a real escort, and that you were giving me a freebie today."

He gave me a thoughtful look. "That does explain why your father was asking me about half-day rates. What did your mom say?"

"My mother knows who you are. She finally recognized you when I said your name. She's not your biggest fan, because that's me, but she watches the show."

"That does explain why she kept staring at me, looking like this." Dalton did a bug-eyed imitation of my mother, frozen in fear yet still smiling to be polite. "What a *lovely* wedding," he said in falsetto. "My niece, Tina, is such a *lovely* bride. Everything is *lovely*."

I cuffed him on the upper arm and attempted to control my laughter. "You're way too good at acting. That's *exactly* what my mother looks like." I wiped the bottom edges of my eyes. "Stop it right now or I'm going to cry and mess up my makeup."

"We wouldn't want that," he said. "Not yet, anyway."

The car pulled up in front of the country club and stopped.

I jumped out. Dalton did as well.

"Thanks for a wonderful date," I said, offering my hand. "I'll remember it forever."

He didn't shake my hand. "Is that all you want from me? Taxi service and a funny anecdote to tell your friends?"

"You've done more than enough to repay me for letting you use the customer washroom at the bookstore."

People who'd been at the church were arriving and entering the building. We were at the Cedars, the prestigious golf and country club. My cousin Tina's new husband, Luca, knew the owner. He'd recently sold the man some vintage motorbikes to help him make a seamless transition into his midlife crisis.

Dalton waved at my parents and Elliot, who'd gotten there ahead of us, then turned and fixed his gaze on me. His expression grew serious, the way it did on *One Vamp to Love*, right before a big plot twist.

"Peaches," he said huskily.

"Dalton," I said, equally huskily.

"Let me come to the reception with you. I'll show you a good time."

"I don't know, Dalton." I shook my head and stepped back. "I've already had enough Torture Bites."

"Torture Bites?" He frowned and gave me a sidelong look. "Is that something from the show? Was it from the early seasons? I'm drawing a blank."

"It's not from the show. A Torture Bite is when someone is eating a delicious dessert and they offer you one tiny little bite. It's cruel. You get a taste, and then you have to sit and suffer while they eat the rest. The taste gets all up inside your mouth, tantalizing you with the torture of pleasure denied."

"Are you implying that I would give you a taste, then deny you the pleasure you deserve?" He stepped forward, his expression hungry. His eyes promised to deny me nothing.

I flung up a hand, palm out, and averted my eyes from the heat as I stepped back. "Easy now. The cameras aren't rolling, Drake Cheshire. You can dial down the smoldering eyes."

"Dial them down? By how much? I do better with specific notes."

"You're at an eleven right now. That's season finale heat. You and I are still in the pilot episode. You should be at a level three, at most."

"Let me try again. How's this?"

I met his gaze tentatively. His expression was at a low simmer.

"This level is okay for me," I said. "I can handle it. But not my mom. Take it down to a two if she manages to make conversation with you."

"So, I'm allowed into the reception?"

"Yes," I said dramatically. "I officially invite you in." I held up a finger. "As my plus one. Not for any weird vampire stuff."

"You do know I'm not an actual vampire."

"Well, let's see when the garlic bread comes around."

We walked into the building, found the reception area in the ballroom, and started mingling. He had his hands in the pockets of his gray slacks most of the time, but was quick to shake hands with the other guests. He looked more comfortable than any of the other men in attendance.

There was a projection screen showing Tina and Luca's engagement photos. Luca was wearing a walking cast on his foot in about half of them. There were a lot of photos.

Dalton watched the slides for a moment then asked, "Why are they posing like depressed catalog models in front of a brick wall?"

"It's what engaged people do. Have you really not been to a regular wedding?"

"I haven't been to a single one. Just the ones on my show." He watched the slideshow some more then said, "Oh, there they are in a wheat field. Okay, well, I like that one. That's a good shot."

In the picture, Tina was lying amongst wildflowers with her head in Luca's lap, gazing skyward.

"That is a good one," I agreed. "She's a florist."

"Her hair is dark, but your mom is blond, and your dad's a redhead. What side is she on?"

"She's my mother's half-sister's daughter. You know what's funny? If you'd been farther up the street, you might have run into her flower shop to hide from those reporters."

"Then everything would have been different," Dalton said.

"True."

The smoldering of his green eyes turned up two notches. "I'm glad I ran into your store."

"It's not mine. I'm just the manager."

"Even so..."

"Refreshments," I said, and steered us over to the bar.

He ordered a light beer, and I got a glass of sparkling white wine.

"A toast," he said. "To your bridesmaid dress, and the way you fill it out."

"Stop teasing me," I said softly, almost whispering.

His eyes locked onto my cleavage. "Speaking of teasing, a guy could drink champagne from there."

I snorted and tugged the bodice up. "Don't be silly. It would drain right through."

"Only one way to find out." He turned toward the bar and raised his fingers to call for the bartender. "Bottle of your best champ—"

I grabbed him by the arm and hauled him away from the bar before he created a huge spectacle.

Tina's other bridesmaids were already staring, mostly at Dalton. They whispered to each other and kept staring. Tina's sister, my other cousin, Megan, caught my eye and made some rude hand gestures then gave me the thumbs-up with her tongue out. Typical Megan.

The Master of Ceremonies tapped a microphone to get everyone's attention. He made a few remarks as we all found our assigned tables, and then he introduced the out-of-town guests.

I thought Dalton would be bored senseless, but he seemed fascinated. "Everything's happening so fast," he kept saying.

Dalton and I were sitting at Table Seven, with a bunch of people I barely knew.

I'd been relieved of my auxiliary bridesmaid duties and shuffled to the Misfits Table, full of tipsy spinsters, people who didn't speak English, and one miserable teenaged boy, who stared at his phone the entire time.

The MC announced that Table Twelve could visit the buffet next. Table Twelve cheered and ran up to get their food.

Dalton leaned over and asked, "Where are those people going?"

"To get first crack at the buffet. We'll go when our number gets called," I explained.

"Is this a normal thing? Do they do this at all weddings?"

"Honestly, I'm not sure," I said. "You can invite my family to a fancy place like the Cedars, but we're just going to do things the regular-people way."

"Interesting," he said.

The MC announced the next table.

I jumped to my feet. "That's us," I said. "We're number seven." I clapped my hands to wake up some of the older spinsters who were nodding off at our table.

As Dalton and I made our way to the buffet, he asked, "Why aren't you sitting at the table with the other bridesmaids?"

"I was a last-minute addition," I explained. "Luca had an old friend from out of town show up, so they needed an extra girl to balance out the guys."

Dalton stopped and stared at the head table. "I think I know that guy," he said. "I know her, too."

"Yes. You saw them get married an hour ago, silly."

"I met them last summer," he said. "I was in the city for a little independent film some friends were shooting. Those two were on the set one night, having a romantic date while we shot an outdoor scene."

"They were extras?"

"Not exactly. They were just watching."

"I heard about that," I said. "Luca invited her to watch a movie, but then he drove past the movie theatre. That was you? What a neat coincidence. Talk about things coming around full circle. You were at their date, and now you're at their wedding."

He gazed into my eyes. "I'm good luck."

I grabbed him by the arms and turned him around. "You'll be bad luck if we miss our shot at the buffet and have to sneak up with another table."

"People do that?"

"I've done it."

He gave me a disapproving look over his shoulder. "You do make bad life choices."

"I get low blood sugar. It's a medical emergency. Sort of."

"You're very quick at justifying your bad life choices."

"Stop judging me and grab a plate."

We started at the end of the buffet.

"This is just like crafty," Dalton said. "Craft services. That's the on-set catering. Here's a tip, in case you're ever working on a production: make friends with whoever's in charge of craft services. They'll give you advance notice when they're putting out the jelly beans, so you can get to them before the grips."

"The grips?"

"Yes. You want to get ahead of the grips. They're the biggest guys on a production, and they ransack the table like Vikings."

I started filling my plate with salad, keenly aware that all the women at the buffet were staring at Dalton. All the men were, too.

Well, of course they were staring. The man was magnificent, like a racehorse.

As he loaded up his plate, I fantasized about brushing his dark-brown, nearly black hair. His hair wasn't very long, but it was thick and slightly wavy.

The last guy I'd dated had been balding with a shaved head, and I used to have dreams about him suddenly sprouting long, bushy hair. Who knew I was so into hair?

My gaze shifted from his gorgeous thoroughbred hair to his green eyes. He was looking right at me. Did he know I had been fantasizing about his hair?

He smiled at me. "What? Is there something in my hair?"

"Nope," I said. "Let's keep it moving along. There are lots of tables waiting. Why are you just standing there?"

He looked down at the buffet and pouted. "Those bread rolls look so good," he moaned. "Someone needs to get between me and those rolls before I do something I regret."

He reached for the rolls in slow motion.

"You're allergic to bread?"

"Not allergic." Eyes wide, still reaching, he said, "Slap my hand away. Do it!"

I slapped his hand anyway.

He moved down the buffet table, his shoulders relaxing as we left the piles of fresh rolls behind.

"Low-carb is tough," he said.

"Tell me about it. That's why I was up on that stool today, putting tape over the vent. I swear Donut Joe's keeps their tastiest donuts right under the cold-air return."

Dalton raised an eyebrow. "That's what you were doing today?"

I rolled my eyes. "No, I was just standing on a stool, hoping some drop-dead gorgeous hunk of a man would come in and catch me in his arms."

"Hunk of a man?"

"That's your last compliment of the evening. You're only here to boost your ego, aren't you?"

"Not true," he said. "My ego is already at maximum size. It can't get boosted any more."

"Then why are you here?"

"Let's call it research."

We reached the end of the buffet and returned to our table.

No sooner had we sat down than people started tapping their cutlery on glasses and chanting, "Kiss, kiss!"

Dalton leaned in toward me. His lips were dangerously close to mine.

"Kiss, kiss, kiss," everyone chanted.

His lips drew closer.

I wanted to kiss him.

"Kiss, kiss, kiss!" The clattering of utensils on glasses reached a crescendo.

We were so close, I could feel the heat of his face radiating onto mine.

I pulled way back.

He gave me a confused look.

"That chanting is for the bride and groom," I said. "Another wedding tradition."

"Are you sure it's not our cue?"

"You're playing dumb with me, aren't you? You know exactly what it means when people at a wedding yell *kiss, kiss, kiss*."

He gave me a hurt look. "Actors are very sensitive about being called dumb. Everyone thinks we're too good-looking to be smart."

"Look." I pointed to Tina and Luca, who were kissing while everyone cheered.

Dalton shook his head and leaned back in his chair. "Show stealers," he said.

"Were you seriously going to kiss me?"

"Yes."

"Wow."

"I was coming on too strong, wasn't I? I can be dramatic sometimes. Hazard of my career. At least I'm not on a cop show, or I'd probably have you in handcuffs."

"I'm not entirely against the idea of kissing you. But handcuffs might be too—"

He moved swiftly, hooking one arm behind my back so I couldn't fall off my chair or get away. Then his lips were on mine, and the kiss felt as right as anything had ever felt right in my life.

Fireworks.

Chapter 4

There were three things I dreaded, besides spiders:

1. Customers at Bookworm Books trying to return books because they didn't like the ending.

2. A long-overdue root canal on my lower-right molar.

3. The end of a date, when everything's going so well, and a disaster is inevitable.

Being at my cousin's wedding had gone from a so-so family obligation to one of the best evenings of my life. Dalton had only kissed me once, but his lips had supernatural powers. That kiss kept me in fireworks mode for hours.

After the speeches and the dances, the wedding festivities gradually wound down. Tina and Luca left on a decorated vintage motorbike. Inside the Cedars' ballroom, the lights came up.

I walked over to say goodnight to my parents, who were gathering their things and preparing to leave. My father had Elliot on his shoulder, fast asleep.

"He looks like such an angel when he's sleeping," I said, then I kissed Elliot on his chubby cheek.

"He's *our* little angel," my mother said, and she gave me a hug. There were tears in her eyes.

"Oh, Mom," I said. "Are you crying again?"

"Weddings make me emotional," she said.

My father looked over at Dalton. The handsome actor was posing for pictures with my cousin Megan, who'd figured out who he was. Megan's boyfriend, the dentist, stood off to the side patiently waiting. Megan's boyfriend was a very patient man, which was good, because he was going to have to wait a lot longer to give me my overdue root canal.

My father said, "This Deangelo fellow seems like a nice young man, for an actor. Everyone's been telling me he's famous. Is that true?"

"It's true," I said. "He's not an A-lister, but people know him. Sorry to break it to you, but he's not a hired escort. I didn't rent him for the evening."

"I figured as much," my father said. "Do you need a ride home?"

"Dalton's driver is going to drop me off."

My parents exchanged a worried look. My father shifted Elliot to his other shoulder.

"Be careful," my mother said.

"Yes," my father said, his expression teasing. "We love Elliot, but we're getting older. We don't have the energy to raise another baby."

"Dad!" I gave him a playful shove, nearly knocking him and Elliot over. "There are people around. What's the point in keeping our family scandal a secret for seven years if you're going to blab about it all over town?"

My mother said, "Your father is just trying to look out for you, Peachy. Be careful with this actor."

"Don't worry," I said in a low tone. "I'm not going to get pregnant, then not know I'm pregnant until I'm suddenly giving birth in the bathtub all alone."

My mother gave me a sad look, as she always did whenever that evening was mentioned. "Your father and I wouldn't have gone away that weekend if we had known."

"Yeah, well, I would have gone in for some prenatal checkups if I had known."

My mother patted Elliot's back. "What's done is done. Our little guy is perfect."

My father leaned in and kissed my cheek. "And so is our little girl. Our perfect peach."

At that moment, Dalton joined us. He shook my parents' hands again and told them it had been a pleasure to be part of the family wedding.

My dad said, "This doesn't need to be your last one. We've got lots of Monroes waiting to be married off."

I said to Dalton, "This from the same man who wanted to rent you for a golf game."

Dalton shrugged. "I'd like to try golf sometime."

"And you shall," my father said confidently. He swayed from side to side. "This kid is getting heavier by the minute. You two have a nice evening. Don't stay up too late." He gave me another peck on my cheek then left with my mother, who kept glancing back at us nervously.

"Your parents are perfect," Dalton said. "The casting director really nailed it."

"Ha ha," I said. "Do you always put things in film and TV lingo?"

"That depends. Do you like it?"

I batted my eyelashes. "I like everything your mouth says, Mr. Drake Cheshire."

"That's *Sir* Drake Cheshire," he said. "I was knighted by the Queen of the Undead in season three."

"Under false pretenses. It hardly counts."

He smiled and glanced over at my parents, who had been stopped at the exit by more relatives.

"How old is your little brother?"

"He's seven," I said.

"That's a big age gap between you two."

I'd heard that comment a hundred times, and my response flowed out as easily as it ever had. "The stork brought my mother a late-in-life surprise, and since the stork wouldn't take him back, they decided to make the most of it."

"I'm happy for you that you have such a nice family." He held out his elbow. "Shall we sneak out that side door? I sent a message to my driver to wake him up."

"Has that poor man been waiting in your car this entire time?"

"It's what he gets paid for," Dalton said.

"Did he get any food?"

"I would imagine he figured out something."

"He needs cake," I said. We swung by the cake table, where wedding cake had been wrapped up for people to take home. I gathered a few pieces, and we made a quick escape through a side exit.

As I prepared to slide into the back seat of the car, I got the feeling I was being watched. I turned my head and saw my father by his car, still holding the boy I'd given birth to.

I felt a chill from the cool night air and shivered. I suddenly had the urge to tell Dalton Deangelo my secret. Elliot Monroe hadn't arrived by the stork, but due to one of my many bad life choices that I was always so quick to justify.

I swallowed down the urge.

What was the point in keeping the family scandal a secret for seven years if I blabbed it to every famous Hollywood actor who gave me a ride in his fancy car?

Chapter 5

It was cozy in the back seat with Dalton at my side.

I didn't want the ride to end. All too quickly, the car reached Baker Street, then the side street, then the tiny rental house I shared with my roommate.

The driver reported to his boss that there didn't seem to be any press lurking around.

Dalton turned to me and said, "Just to be safe, I should kiss you goodnight here in the car."

"That doesn't sound very safe to me."

"I'll keep it family friendly."

"Like in the movies?"

"Like in the movies." His voice low, barely audible, he asked, "Do you want me to give you a dramatic on-screen kiss?"

"I kinda do."

Dalton's expression got ultra-serious. He transformed into Drake Cheshire, the cultured vampire with a taste for big-lipped girls under one hundred pounds. He stared intensely at my eyes, my lips, my cleavage, my throat, my lips, and then up to my eyes again. I melted like a pat of butter on summer pavement.

He moved in closer, so our noses were an inch apart, and he repeated the intense look. Eyes. His, green like precious emeralds. Mine, unable to blink. Lips. His, gorgeous. Mine, slightly parted and trembling. Throat. Mine, feeling very exposed. Cleavage. Mine, heaving, probably, guessing by the way I couldn't quite catch my breath.

His gaze slid back dreamily to my lips, and he tilted his head to the side, not yet touching his mouth to mine.

We held steady. I could feel the heat from his skin against my lips. He tipped his head back and looked me in the eyes again.

Oh, the slow torture.

His lips grazed mine for an instant, then he pulled back way too soon.

That was it?

He asked, "Would you like me to walk you to your door?"

"Sure. Maybe you can give me the other three-quarters of that kiss."

"Maybe."

I pushed open my door and climbed out of the car as gracefully as I could manage, considering I couldn't feel my legs at all.

It was past midnight. A few people were out in the neighborhood, walking their dogs. The dog walkers stared our way. They were only looking at the unusual car, but the paranoid part of me was certain they could sense how I was feeling.

"Cute house," Dalton said.

"It's not much to look at, but it's cheap, and it's got a big porch. Nisha promised our landlord we were going to paint the whole thing. Doug said to go for it, and he'd pay for the supplies, but then all we managed to do was paint the front door. Whenever you see people painting a house in a movie montage, it looks like fun, but in real life, it's grueling."

"I wouldn't know," Dalton said. "I've only done the movie version, where you hold the paintbrush against a dry wall, then have a paint fight with your friends."

We walked up to the front door. Was he expecting me to invite him in? I did want to, in spite of my mother's warnings.

I fumbled around in my purse for my keys.

Dalton put his arm around my shoulders and whispered, "Don't look now, but there's a photographer behind that tree."

I whispered back, "What should I do?"

"Are those real or fake potted plants on the steps?"

"They're real. They're geraniums."

"How do you water them? Is there a hose at the front of the house?"

Still whispering, I said, "Yes. It's coiled up right behind that hedge."

"Go turn on the water for the hose. Make up some dialog."

"You mean improvise? Like an actor?"

He grinned. "Yes, Peaches. Improvise."

Loudly, for the sneaky photographer to hear, I said, "Just a minute. I need to check on the garden." I went down the steps and stepped onto the lawn. The grass tickled the sides of my feet through my sandals.

"It's a lovely lawn," he said, just as loud.

"We don't use any herbicides, so I'm out here on my hands and knees pulling weeds all the time."

There was movement along the sides of the tree. I saw an elbow, a shadowy head, and a camera.

I bent down to turn on the water, feeling indignant that someone was taking my photo without my permission. The wedding photographer had been annoying, but this was way beyond that.

Dalton already had the business end of the hose in hand. Clutching the sprayer like a pistol, he crept closer to the big tree.

I gave him a nod. The water was on. *Do it.*

He fired one small shot of water at the hedge to test, then ran around to the other side of the tree, the water on full blast.

The person he ambushed let out a high-pitched shriek.

I'd expected a male paparazzi, or maybe the redheaded woman I'd seen earlier at the bookstore. Instead, what jumped out from behind the tree, as mad and wet as a Persian cat in a bathtub, was a woman. She looked twenty-something, with dark hair in a short pixie cut. She was tiny, and as cute as a teacup full of buttons.

He stopped blasting the water. "Josie? Why are you following me?"

The petite woman—Josie—sputtered and wiped at her face dramatically.

"Don't you dare spray me again," she said, breathing heavily.

"Or what?"

As she opened her mouth to answer, he fired off a blast of water at her midsection.

She howled in outrage.

Lights flicked on in my neighbors' houses. Shadows moved in windows.

Josie cursed, then yelled at Dalton, "You're such a child! You're a spoiled rotten baby! You don't care who gets hurt because you'll just move on to the next one, and women are in unlimited supply, aren't we? You've got your new girl here, and you probably fed her your stupid lines, didn't you?"

"Josie, calm down. Are you following me? Is this what you do now?"

Growling with sarcasm, she said, "No, I have an amazing career. Six seasons and a movie. I'm a big deal, and I only sell celebrity photos for giggles." She raised her camera at him and said, "Huh, it still works." A red light blinked, then the camera flashed.

Dalton stepped toward her, one hand outstretched. "Give me that. I'm deleting these photos. You have no right."

She backed away, still taking pictures. "Work it, D-man. Gimme that Drake snarl. Oh yeah, action shot."

"Talk to me, Josie. Do you need money? I can help you, as a friend, but you're not being very friendly."

She abruptly changed direction and started running straight toward me.

I reacted the same way I would have if a skunk or saber tooth tiger had been running at me. I froze and held very still, hoping she'd lose interest.

The wet woman grabbed my forearm, her chilly fingers digging in. "You don't know what you're getting yourself into," she snarled in my face.

I snapped out of terror mode. "Let go of me right now before I punch you some new freckles."

She blinked, speechless. She'd probably never had anyone threaten to punch her some new freckles. In fact, it may have been the first time in human history that phrase had been uttered.

"Who are you?" she asked, her eyes open wide.

"Just a girl named Peaches."

"You have phenomenal skin."

"Why, thank you—"

Our conversation was interrupted by a man tackling Josie and throwing her to the ground.

It was Dalton's driver, who was apparently also a bodyguard.

Dalton came to my side and put one arm across my shoulders. "Are you okay?"

"Don't worry about me. Call your guard dog off that tiny girl."

The driver had already pulled away from Josie, camera in hand.

Even though nobody was touching the girl, she continued to scream bloody blue murder with cheese on top.

All my curious neighbors were out on their porches.

Mr. Galloway called down from next door, "Peaches Monroe? Are you in trouble? Shall I call the police?"

I waved. "No need, Mr. Galloway. We're just having some fun."

He stayed at the railing, motionless. "Is that a bridesmaid dress you're wearing, or did someone invite you to prom?"

"It's a bridesmaid dress. My cousin Tina got married today."

"Oh, really? Was it a big wedding?"

Some people in the city complained they didn't know their neighbors. I couldn't say the same. My neighbors were born to be neighborly. They spent nine out of ten Sundays digging around in their front yards for no reason other than to be available for chats.

I answered Mr. Galloway. "Not too big. Maybe a hundred people. It was up at the Cedars."

He nodded. "Good weather for it." He gave me a salute then returned to his house.

I turned around to see how the skirmish was going. I was hit in the face with a blast of cold water. Someone had turned the hose on me. I yelped and tried to take cover. I bumped into people who were also yelling. I grabbed someone, and we both fell to the ground. The hose-blasting stopped.

I looked up to see the petite woman, Josie, making her getaway down the street.

I tried to get up, but I was pinned underneath Dalton Deangelo. Talk about a dream come true! I'd fantasized many times about having him on top of me, but not like that. Not in the mud on my front lawn. Or maybe in the mud, sure, but not with all my neighbors watching.

The driver/bodyguard picked up Dalton then helped me to my feet.

Dalton said, "I am so sorry about... Josie." In the dim light, I couldn't tell if he was more guilty or embarrassed.

I looked down at my muddy bridesmaid dress. "So much for wearing this dress again."

"I'll pay to have it cleaned. No. I'll buy you a new dress. Unfortunately, if you hang out with me, this is the sort of thing that happens."

"Your life must be very interesting. I'd love to trade with you for a day."

He pursed his lips, his green eyes twinkling at me. "Give me the keys, and I'll go work at the bookstore tomorrow."

"You would mess up everything," I said. "I have Bookworm Books exactly how I like it."

He brushed his hands along my upper arms, sweeping away the beads of water on my skin. His hands were surprisingly warm, yet I shivered at his touch.

"Making a mess can be fun," he said.

I noticed he didn't explain who Josie was, or why she had warned me to stay away from him.

"Thanks for everything, but I should go inside before I catch a summer cold."

I gave him a peck on the cheek, then ran up to my house and inside.

I did not invite the two-hundred-year-old TV vampire known as Drake Cheshire into my home.

Not that night, anyway.

Chapter 6

The morning after my cousin Tina's wedding and my date with Dalton Deangelo, I did not wake up alone. Not if you count my laptop.

I pulled my trusty laptop out from under my shoulder and cracked it open tentatively. What trouble had I gotten into the night before? Drinking and online shopping were a bad combination for me.

After the whole ordeal on the lawn with Dalton, his bodyguard, and that angry Josie girl, I'd come inside and told my roommate everything. Then she had poured me a drink or two to settle my nerves before bed. Make that a drink or *five*.

The last time I'd had five drinks and woken up with my laptop, I'd discovered I was the new owner of an authentic German cuckoo clock. It had showed up at my door the next day and, like the hangover, was nonrefundable.

Since I already owned an authentic German cuckoo clock, I wondered what new thing might have caught my drunken fancy the night before.

I opened my email to find a bunch of confirmation messages.

Apparently, I'd joined an official Dalton Deangelo fan club. An adrenaline blast of horror shot through me, making my brain throw up inside my head.

I closed the laptop to keep the awful truth quiet, then laughed at myself. Dalton was a huge star. He probably had high-priced people who had medium-priced people to deal with his fan clubs. Maybe his driver/bodyguard ran things while he was waiting in the car for his client.

My bedroom door creaked open. My roommate and best friend, Nisha Patel, meandered in, eyes half-lidded. The smell of incense wafted in with her, as always. Nisha was always meditating, or cleansing her aura, or doing something mystical that involved burning things or warming oils.

"Timber," she said before falling onto the bed next to me. "It's not *remotely fair* that you should still be asleep when I'm awake and bored."

I moaned.

She said, "You don't sound very chuffed about the fact that it's Sunday, and neither of us has to work."

Nisha spoked with her adorable English accent—the one that hadn't gone away, even though her family had left England when she was twelve. The day she showed up at my school, everyone was so curious about the Indian girl with the British accent. Some of the boys teased her, calling her Nisha Papadum instead of Nisha Patel. She dealt with it by bringing fresh papadums to school and distributing them at lunch time. After that, it was uncool for anyone to tease her about her background.

We had become friends immediately—the tasty papadams hadn't hurt—and best friends not long after that.

She poked me in the cheek. "What's wrong? Are you coming down from the high of your date with Dalton Deangelo? Has your life gone *all to pot*?"

"Something like that," I said. "Can you be heartbroken over someone you only spent a few hours with?"

"You can be heartbroken over someone you never met. I'm still upset about an extremely vivid dream I had over a year ago, and that was just a dream." She waved her hands around me. "Do you want me to do a cleansing ritual on your aura?"

"No need for your witchcraft just yet," I said. Nisha had studied the spiritual works of her ancestors, but her interests in the otherworldly were not limited to India. She'd recently gone through an intense Wiccan phase, and was also interested in voodoo. But not in a scary, bite-the-heads-off-live-chickens sort of way. She wasn't the type to do curses. Her interest was mostly expressed through the purchasing of various scented candles.

"It's not witchcraft," she said. "Go to the kitchen and eat a raw egg plus some raw cabbage. That'll help your hangover."

"No need," I said quickly. "I'm feeling better already." The prospect of eating a raw egg and cabbage really was magical.

"I'll buy you a hug. Get ready." She threw one arm and one long leg over my body.

I sighed and patted her head, enjoying the feel of her silky black hair. Nisha had the best hair. She used a shampoo for show ponies. The product didn't do anything impressive for me and my delicate blond locks, but Nisha could have been its spokesperson.

Actually, she could have been the spokesperson for anything. Nisha Patel was stunning, from the nail beds of her always-pedicured toes to her full, naturally ruby-hued lips and her golden eyes. Her skin was brown and perfectly clear, and her smile was dazzling. Her secret shame was her unusually large feet. She claimed to wear a size ten shoe, but if you caught hold of her new pairs of shoes, before she'd filed away or peeled off the size, you'd find the number eleven or twelve.

"Thanks for the hug," I said, struggling as I got free of her passive embrace.

"Hit the shower," she said. "That workshop starts in one hour."

"What workshop?"

"The one you agreed to come with me to last night, between drinks three and four."

"Was it a workshop for rolling sushi?" My mouth watered at the idea of cool cucumber slices.

Her voice flat, Nisha said, "Yeah. Rolling sushi."

"I want sushi."

"There's no sushi. It's a workshop for women, silly. We're going to learn how to be captivating, and have men wrapped around our fingers."

"I'd rather have sushi."

"Sushi doesn't get you kissed in the back seat by a famous actor while a chauffeur drives you around." She sat up and looked me in the eyes. "Are you sure you only kissed? You got home pretty late."

"We *barely* kissed."

"Because you were...?"

I hit her with a pillow.

"No time for pillow fights," she said. "Shower now. Light the purple candle while you're in there. Make sure you get the mud out of your ears. You can't learn the secrets of womanly charm with mud in your ears."

"Purple candle. Wash off mud. Gotcha." I finished extracting myself from the covers.

Nisha jumped up from my bed and grabbed the top novel off a stack of books. "This looks good." She flipped to the end and started reading the last page.

I grabbed the paperback away. "Stop it."

She grabbed it back and resumed reading.

I tackled her to the ground. We rolled around on the fluffy rug next to my bed.

"You're so weird about your books," she said, breathing heavily and trying to wrestle the book back.

"Books are supposed to be read from front to back. I'm not weird. You're weird."

She stopped flailing for a moment. "Why would I waste my time reading a book if I'm going to hate the ending?"

I got the book away from her and chucked it out my open window.

She wriggled out from underneath me and got up. "Hit the shower now or never. We're going to this workshop. You need to learn how to be a lady."

"You need to learn how to read a book."

She waved her hand dismissively as she went off to finish applying essential oils.

Chapter 7

The workshop was at the local community center.

We arrived on time, thanks to Nisha's time-management skills. We'd reached a compromise on her raw-egg-and-cabbage hangover cure and made scrambled eggs with ketchup and sauerkraut. I did feel a lot better.

The class was in a multi-purpose room with musical instruments on the wall and child-sized furniture pushed to the side. We sat in stackable chairs, arranged in a circle. At the corner of the room was a cloth screen that nude models used to disrobe behind for live drawing events.

I'd been there before. Nisha had dragged me to a few live drawing classes with nude models. The instructor was the mother of our friend, Sunshine Banks. Mrs. Banks was encouraging, and a great art teacher. Nisha and I had enjoyed drawing naked people, but the novelty had faded after a few sessions, and we hadn't gone back.

We took our seats and looked around the group. Seated across from me was an acquaintance, Rhonda. She worked at Donut Joe's and made my coffee the way I liked it. We said hello.

The workshop instructor, Dottie, sailed into the room in gauzy layers.

She did a head count—there were thirty-three of us ladies, all ages—and started the session.

Dottie said, "My name is Dottie Simpkins, and my age is not what you'd guess. I drive a convertible with a bumper sticker that says 'If the sun's up, the top's down.' I've been married six times. If you take all my advice today, I guarantee you can cut that number in half, minimum."

The ladies gathered in the circle giggled.

Dottie asked, "How many of you have read my New York Times Bestseller book, *The Secret Rules of Love*?"

A few hands went up.

I leaned over and whispered to Nisha, "My cousin Megan is obsessed with that book."

She whispered back, "You should read it."

Dottie set up an easel that held a number of poster-sized cards and flipped over the front one to reveal a drawing of a mermaid. "Lesson number one: Keeping your legs together."

Nisha shot me an apologetic look. "I'm sorry, Peaches," she whispered. "I thought this workshop was supposed to be sex positive."

Dottie stopped the class and said to Nisha, "Young lady, I may have more white hairs than all of you put together, but my hearing is excellent. I'll have you know this is a very sex-positive workshop." She waved at the drawing of the mermaid. "We begin with the mermaid lesson because it's meaningful when a mermaid sprouts legs. In every tale, the transformation represents a sacrifice or gift, and it is something to be honored."

Nisha put her palms together and gave Dottie one of her yoga bows.

Dottie smiled to show the apology was accepted. Then the spunky older lady looked around the room of women. "Any other comments or questions, or shall we begin?"

Dead silence.

She resumed the workshop.

Charm, as Dottie explained it through an assortment of metaphors and fairy tales, was about using your feminine talents while embracing your individuality.

For example, to draw a man to you, you stood or sat in such a way that one toe pointed at him. That would lure him in. Then, when he got near your trap, you were to gaze up at him like he was a strawberry sundae while stroking the parts of your body you wanted to draw attention to.

I raised my hand and asked, "What part do I rub to draw attention to my brains?"

Nisha huddled into me and snickered into my shoulder.

Dottie didn't miss a beat. "Honey, with your hourglass figure, I'd suggest you stick to the chest. The brains can be a bonus down the road." Then she moved on to the next question.

At the end of the workshop, Dottie said, "As the great Oscar Wilde says, be yourself, because everyone else is already taken." She paused for dramatic effect. "Ladies, every one of us is a role model. We just don't know yet for whom."

The class applauded. Dottie handed out cards for her other business, a natural beeswax candle company called Mind Your Beeswax.

Nisha and I left the class and practiced our mermaid walk on the way back to Nisha's car.

"How's this?" Nisha asked. "Am I a mermaid?"

She was walking the way Dottie had taught us, with her upper legs close together, like she was wearing an invisible tight skirt instead of jean cutoffs with frayed edges.

"It looks like you're putting in a lot of effort," I said.

Nisha gave me a frustrated look. "Isn't that the point?"

"You have to try harder to look like you're not trying." I handed her my purse and sashayed down the sidewalk with my upper legs together. "Like this."

"You look like you're trying to hold onto a credit card with your bum cheeks."

"Well, that *is* where I keep my emergency credit card."

"Forget the mermaid walk," Nisha said. "How are my sexy wardrobe adjustments?" She was wearing a striped shirt with a wide neck. She casually shrugged, allowing the shirt to fall off one shoulder, then deliberately ran her finger across her smooth brown collarbone before pulling the shirt back up.

"Super hot," I said. "Marry me."

"Now you do it," she said.

Dottie had recommended wearing high-maintenance clothing that required constant adjustment. Men were attracted to women who were constantly correcting their clothing, or so Dottie said.

Staring intensely into Nisha's beautiful golden eyes, I reached down, plucked a pebble from my cork-soled sandals, then blew on the pebble suggestively before tossing it aside.

Nisha said, "I'm not sure that's what Dottie meant about adjusting your clothes."

"How about this?" I reached into my khakis and tugged my underwear back into place.

"That was the opposite of alluring," Nisha said. "Unsettling, even."

"But it feels so good to pull your underwear down when it's riding up," I said, giving it a second adjustment. "Why doesn't anyone make cute underwear for curvy girls?"

"Lots of companies do," Nisha said. "You would know if you ever went shopping for clothes. You'd rather spend your money on books and keep wearing the cheap underwear your mom gives you for Christmas."

"I'm not paying top dollar for something nobody but me is going to see."

"Dottie says you need to invest in yourself."

"Dottie has been married six times. Just because someone has made all the mistakes doesn't mean they have the answers."

Nisha looked over my shoulder at something. Her pretty, naturally ruby-red mouth dropped open.

"Hot buttered noodles," she said. "Is that Adrian Stromquist? Is he back in town?"

I whipped my head around so fast the bells on my earrings jingled.

Nisha was right. Hot buttered noodles, indeed. Adrian Stromquist was back in town, and he was right there, in the community center parking lot. The tall, handsome, Nordic-looking man had changed since the last time I'd seen him, but I recognized him instantly.

Back in high school, I'd been the president, secretary, and only member of the Adrian Stromquist Appreciation Club.

Adrian had been tall then, too, but scrawny. Our English teacher joked that the metal ring in his lip was the only thing keeping him from blowing away in a stiff breeze. Teenaged Adrian had worn extra-large black T-shirts for his favorite bands—shirts so big you could have fit two Adrians in them. I used to note the names of the bands and listen to their music as though Adrian had recommended them to me personally. His favorite band of all time was a classic rock group called Megasoystick. He used to rave about how they were unappreciated because everyone thought they'd ripped off more popular rock bands, but if you went through their catalog, it was obvious that the borrowing had gone the other way.

Nisha grabbed my elbow and squeezed it. "This is exactly what Dottie said would happen," she said. "After we did our meditation, I focused on manifesting true love for you, and now here he is."

"Manifest your own stuff. Don't get your manifesting mojo mixed up with mine. It's not right."

"I did it," Nisha said excitedly, like the willing believer she was. "I manifested Adrian Stromquist. Right out of the blue." She looked at her hands in wonder. "I've got powers."

"It's just a coincidence, you superstitious, new-age nutbar."

"Dottie says there's no such thing as coincidences." Nisha turned me around and pushed me toward Adrian with her hand on the small of my back. "You have to talk to him."

"I don't *have to* do anything."

She gave me another shove. "You should have declared your undying love for him back when you two were in the yearbook committee together, working those late hours, just the two of you. But you missed your chance, and he started dating Sunshine Banks."

I grumbled, "They weren't really dating. They were just friends."

"Now he's back in town, and you've got a second chance." She gave me another push.

I whipped around. "Shove me again and I'll take you down, woman. This morning's book tussle was just a warmup act."

"You don't get it," Nisha said, her golden eyes glowing with excitement. "But I do. This is mythical, what's happening right now. Adrian Stromquist is the call to adventure."

"What's happening is you need a snack. We both need a snack. That workshop was exhausting."

"Don't you get it? You're the hero, and you're refusing the call, because that's what heroes always do, until something forces them into action. I learned all about it at last week's workshop. Or was it two weeks ago?"

I stared at my best friend. "Nisha, is there a self-development workshop at the community center you won't take?"

"I'm a knowledge seeker," she said. "The hero always refuses the first call, because they don't want to change. Nobody ever wants to change, because it's uncomfortable. Outside events have to point them in the right direction."

"Nisha, you know I'm perfectly fine with being uncomfortable. You think I wear these cute little cork-soled sandals for comfort?"

She ignored my point. "It's my sacred duty to point you in the right direction."

"Shove me again, and I will melt all your chakra candles into one hideous super-candle."

Nisha stepped to the side, put her fingers in her mouth, and let out a loud whistle.

"Adrian!" She waved to get his attention. "Yes, I'm talking to you, Adrian Stromquist! It's me, Nisha Patel, and your girl, Peaches. Remember us?"

Chapter 8

Adrian Stromquist heard Nisha, and he started walking our way.

He was one tall drink of water, and he got even taller as he drew nearer. Adrian had a long, rectangular face and angular features under sun-bleached fair hair and fair eyebrows. His eyes were pale blue, hooded and deep set.

"Look at you two," he said. "Nisha and Peaches. It's like a high school reunion." He glanced up at the community center behind us. "What are you doing here?"

"We did a workshop," Nisha said.

He gazed at us intently, a vaguely mocking grin on his lips. "Yeah? On what?" I remembered that look. Adrian was a smart guy, and he always asked questions as a lead-in to mocking someone.

I beat him to the punch by not giving him a straight answer. I said, "It was a workshop for ladies only, about how to draw men into our traps."

He gave me an amused look, his eyes still mocking. "Something tells me you don't need to take a workshop on that."

My cheeks flushed. I'd walked right into that, despite knowing it was a trap.

I dropped my gaze from his piercing pale-blue eyes to his lips. In the indentation below his lower lip was the tiniest knob of scar tissue from where teenaged Adrian's stainless steel lip ring had been. The one that I used to fantasize about nibbling on myself.

"You took out your piercing," I said.

"A while back," he said. "I didn't need the extra weight to keep me from blowing away or slipping down the shower drain." He turned to the side, raised an arm, and flexed his bicep for us. I quickly glanced away, pretending to be uninterested.

"You're looking so fit and healthy," Nisha said, twisting her upper body and making her wide-necked striped shirt fall off her shoulder again.

Adrian said to her, "Looks like you got the wrong size shirt, Nisha. This one keeps trying to get away from you." He used his fingertips to lift and center the shirt for her. "Much better."

"It's supposed to do that," Nisha said, pulling the shirt to the side again before sweeping her delicate fingers across her bare skin.

Adrian turned to me. Although he was irritating, with his mocking, know-it-all attitude, the full force of his gorgeousness nearly knocked me down in my hungover, post-workshop, confused state.

He said, "I used to wear shirts that were way too big. Remember that, Peaches?"

"I remember," I said. "It looks like you finally grew into your collection. You're all bumpy now."

"Bumpy?" He flexed again. "I guess I shouldn't be surprised to hear you call me bumpy, Peaches. What else is new? Your mouth never did wait for your brain to send orders." He looked me over, those dazzling blue eyes roving down my body slowly, seeking every valley like a summer rainstorm. "You're one to talk," he said. "I see some bumps in all the right places."

I crossed my arms over my chest. "My eyes are up here. Stop eye-groping my peaches."

Adrian chuckled, his chiseled cheeks taking on a rosy glow.

He asked, "What are you two up to these days?"

"Yoga studio," Nisha said. "I do everything. I'm basically the manager, but I don't get paid management rates."

"That's on you," Adrian said. "How about you, Peaches?"

"Working at Bookworm Books. My parents are disappointed I'm not taking the corporate world by storm."

"The corporate world is overrated." Adrian lowered his gaze and bowed his head, his long, fair eyelashes nearly brushing his cheeks. "I guess I should just come right out and admit the awful truth."

Nisha said, "Your energy... You're all blocked up. What's wrong, Adrian?"

"I'm broke," he said.

"Join the club," I replied.

"That explains it," Nisha said. "But being broke is just a temporary state. You're not *broken*."

"I may be broken as well," he said softly.

I reached up—way up—for his shoulder and squeezed it. "Oh, Adrian. You're too big and stubborn to be broken. Don't say that."

"Tell that to my parents. I moved back in with them."

My heart skipped a beat. "You're back for good? Not just visiting?"

He turned and looked off into the distance, his expression forlorn. He had always been a moody guy. I'd called him Stormy Weather Adrian for a reason.

He said gloomily, "So much for all my big plans. I thought I had the world by the tail, but I made a few bad investments and then went double or nothing and came out with nothing." He shook his head. "Real estate. A person might as well go to Vegas and play the roulette wheel."

Nisha darted forward, smacking him on the broad chest with both hands. "Snap out of it!"

He gave her a stunned look, as though she'd blasted him with defibrillation paddles. He took two staggering steps backward then asked me, "Was Nisha always this...?"

"Maniacal? Yes," I said. "Maybe she wasn't like this with you back in high school, but she's always trying to clear my energy fields."

Nisha shook her fingers at Adrian, ignoring me as she delivered a lecture. "Stop feeling sorry for yourself, Adrian Stromquist. You're the same age as us, and we're all broke. I've never been to a party that wasn't bring-your-own-bottle. You're so freaking handsome now, and you need to stop complaining. You used to be skinny and weird back in high school, and nobody but Peaches took much notice of you, but now you're back, and look at you. You could be the mayor of this city, if you wanted."

Adrian slowly nodded. "I always liked you, Nisha. You make a lot of sense." He turned to me and smiled that know-it-all grin, his eyes teasing. "And you, Peaches. You were trouble in high school, but I always liked you, too."

"Thanks for that," I said flatly. "I wouldn't have gotten into nearly as much trouble if it wasn't for you."

He narrowed his eyes and said nothing.

"We should hang out," Nisha said. "All of us. Like old times."

He bobbed his head. "Yeah. We should totally get together with the old gang. It's been five years since graduation, so we could call it our official five-year reunion."

Nisha clapped her hands. "We could have the party at our house."

Adrian's sun-bleached eyebrows rose. "You two bought a house together?"

"We're just renting," I said. "Calm your real estate lust. We're not property moguls."

"Neither am I," Adrian said moodily. "Not anymore."

"There he is," I said, pointing at his long torso. "Moody, pouty Adrian. You've put on a few pounds of beefcake, but you're still the same mopey teenager, muttering about how nobody understands you and nobody gets the brilliance of Megasoystick."

Adrian stared at me.

Nisha elbowed me. "Be nice to Adrian. Let's not fall into our old high school patterns. I hated being around you two bickering over everything like an old married couple."

"Yeah," Adrian said, lifting his chin and looking down his long nose at me. "Be nice to me. Don't fall into your old pattern of being cruel to me, Peaches."

"Me?" I held my hand to my chest. "You're the one who was always..." My whole body was vibrating. I was too upset to finish my thought, which was something that rarely happened.

"Group hug," Nisha said cheerfully. She forced us into a hug entanglement.

"Careful," I muttered into Adrian's armpit area. "The giant ogre people need to watch where they're putting their pointy elbows."

Adrian patted me on the back before pulling away.

"Well," he said, looking at me and not smiling. "This has been interesting."

Nisha handed him her phone. "Put your number in." She shot me a dirty look then smiled up at our old friend. "I never know what's going on with you two, but you need to clear that old energy so we can have fun like we did in the old days. We are definitely going to hang out this summer. All three of us."

Adrian put his number into her phone, then got hers for his phone. He handed me his phone.

I gave him a warning look. "I'll give you my number, but you'd better not send me any gross pictures of Brazil."

"Brazil?" He gave me a blank look.

Nisha explained, "When you get your legs waxed, it's called leg waxing. When you get your bathing suit area done, it's called a Brazilian. Therefore, that means *this* is Brazil." She waved at the general area of his jeans.

"Ah. The rainforests of Brazil. I should have guessed," Adrian said. "You two are like those weird twins who invent their own language."

Together, Nisha and I said, "Thank you!"

Chapter 9

Monday, May 9th

I did the author and workshop presenter Dottie Simpkins' sexy mermaid walk on the way in to work Monday morning. I let my thighs rub together. Who was I kidding? Given my figure, there was no way to walk *without* my thighs rubbing together. But, like a mermaid, I did keep my knees close together and my weight back over my heels so that ants could run parades under my relaxed toes.

I was in the mood for a mocha, so I walked into Donut Joe's that way.

Rhonda looked up from the cafe latte she was steaming. "Peaches, do you have a bladder infection?" Rhonda wasn't young, but she had the deep, gravelly voice of a much older woman. "Why are you walking like that?"

I relaxed and took a comfortable, wider stance. "Just trying to have more charm. Probably a lost cause."

Rhonda pointed at me knowingly. "Dottie's mermaid walk. Good for you. I forgot everything that woman said the minute I walked out of there."

"Why do we go to those things?"

Rhonda shrugged. "Beats me. What else are you supposed to do on Sunday morning?"

From behind me, a male voice said, "I hear snuggling and doing the crossword puzzle is nice."

I whirled around, expecting to see another regular customer.

It wasn't a regular customer, let alone a regular person.

Dalton Deangelo, the famous actor, sat at a round cafe table. He had a laptop in front of him and a foamy cappuccino next to it.

"You," I said, pointing.

"It's me," he said, grinning. The dimple in his chin deepened.

"You're here."

Dalton narrowed his emerald-green eyes. "I think so. Wait, what were we talking about? Line?" He looked left and right playfully. "I'm lousy when I go off-script."

I walked over to his table. "What are you doing here at Donut Joe's?"

He pointed his thumb at the wall behind him. "Waiting for the bookstore next door to open."

What was he doing there? He was going to ruin everything. I'd already had my once-in-a-lifetime date with the actor. Everything had been perfect. If he kept coming around, and I got to know him better, I'd only find out he was a horrible jerk and unworthy of my affection. I'd eventually hate him, like that Josie girl.

Maybe if I ignored him, he'd go away.

I turned back to the counter to place my order with Rhonda.

I casually asked her, "How are things?"

"The usual," Rhonda said in her gravelly voice. "I think that guy you were talking to is some sort of actor."

"He is," I said.

"Do you know him?"

"Can you ever *really* know an actor? They're always feeding you lines."

Dalton interjected, "I can hear you. I'm only five feet away."

I said to Rhonda, "And they're so nosy. They think everything's about them."

"Narcissists," she said. "I know the type. You want the usual? Mocha?"

"Yes, please." I glanced over my shoulder at Dalton. His mug was empty. "Hey, actor guy," I said. "Want me to buy you a refill?"

He gave me a surprised look. "Sure. Get it in a paper cup. I have business next door."

"You heard the pretty boy," I said to Rhonda.

"He is pretty," she said. "Does he play a warlock on TV?"

"Vampire," I said.

Rhonda cackled. "Careful he doesn't bite you on the neck."

I kept a poker face. Most of my fantasies about Drake Cheshire *did* involve him biting me on the neck. Repeatedly and without mercy.

Rhonda made both drinks. I handed them to Dalton, and we went next door to the bookstore.

My hands were shaking as I tried to open up. I felt like I was in a horror movie, trying to get into my car before the vampire swooped down and bit me. I dropped the keys.

Dalton picked up the keys and handed them to me.

"I'm in town shooting another indie movie," he said.

"I hadn't asked, but that's cool." I tried again with the keys, keeping my back to him. "How long?" I tried to sound casual, but it came out sounding like a squeaky gate.

I dropped the keys again.

He scooped up the keys and opened the door for me.

"Long enough to get bored and look for trouble," he said.

"I'm sure trouble finds you easily enough on its own."

We stepped inside the shop. I left him at the door and ran to turn off the alarm. As I flipped on the lights, I heard him breathe in deeply.

"Can't beat that smell," he said. "Heaven is a place on earth, and it's a bookstore."

"We have some bookmarks that say that."

"I know." He held up the bookmark he must have been reading from.

"You and your scripts," I said. "Why are you hanging out here on Baker Street on a Monday morning? Isn't shooting a movie kind of an intense, all-day thing?"

"I've got today off because I'm not the main role in this one. The other lead is the one with the big transformation. It's very inspiring."

I got myself behind the counter, where I felt more comfortable, half hidden.

"You're not the star? Then why are you doing it?"

"Because I get to play a complex character and do some serious acting. I don't mean to bite the hand that feeds me, but spewing out corny dialog around prosthetic fangs is not the reason I fought my way into this business."

"What's the movie called?"

"The working title is *Waterfall*, but that's not the final title. You've probably seen arrow signs around town with the word *Waterfall* on them."

"Have I?" I took a sip of my mocha.

"You will now, since I told you."

"Honestly, I don't know much about how movies get made."

"That gives us plenty to talk about." He gave me a sexy look, his emerald-green eyes full of intensity. "I had a really nice time with you Saturday."

I took another sip, noting how flavorless the mocha was. Stress will do that to you—suck the taste right out of your mouth. Dalton was handsome and charming, but every minute he was around me was putting us a minute closer to me finding out what was wrong with him.

"I'm not going to blab to any reporters, if that's what you're worried about," I said. "I won't tell anyone about meeting you."

He leaned forward in a deliberate pose of relaxation against the counter, elbows on the countertop and chin in hand. Raising one sexy, dark eyebrow, he gazed into my eyes and said, "Tell the world."

"I told my roommate," I said. "Plus my whole extended family saw you at the wedding."

"I've got nothing to hide," he said.

I bit my tongue. People who said that always did.

"Dinner tonight?" he asked. "Unless you're mad at me for getting mud on your bridesmaid dress."

"I don't care about the dress."

The front door bells jingled with customers coming in.

"I should let you get to work." He drummed on the counter top. "Dinner tonight? Pick you up here or at home?"

"What about your stalker? Josie? Will she be joining us tonight, too?"

His expression clouded. "I hope not. I believe that situation has been taken care of."

More customers came in.

Dalton said, "Busy place." He picked up the green tea I'd bought him. "See you tonight. Bernard will pick you up at your house at seven o'clock."

Before I could say anything, he added, "Bernard is my driver. He really appreciated the wedding cake, by the way. It was very thoughtful, and not in a Hollywood way. He says you're a keeper."

Then he left.

Chapter 10

I was so nervous about my date with Mr. Sexy-mouth Vampire-charm that I couldn't figure out what to wear, so I sat on a pile of clothes and bawled my face off.

Nisha came running to my bedroom. "Is somebody torturing a small mammal in here?"

"Not a small mammal. Not small at all." I picked up a pair of sky-blue jeans and tossed them at her. "Why did you let me buy these? One wash and they've shrunk to the size of doll clothes."

"Oh, no."

"Nisha, please go grab the slipcover off the sofa and cut a neck hole in it, because that's what I'll be wearing tonight."

She crossed her arms, no pity in her golden eyes at all. "Poor Peaches. She has a dinner date with a hot actor. Why are you acting like this? It's not your moon cycle yet."

"Mind your own business about my moon cycle." I pouted harder.

"I don't understand why you're not happy about recent developments," she said. "Most girls would kill to switch places with you. Since we saw Adrian Stromquist yesterday, I've been thinking that he's your big adventure, but maybe Dalton is the one. Why are you so miserable?"

"I told you. Dalton Deangelo is perfect inside my head. But he's just a human being. He's going to do something hideous, and then I won't have him anymore."

"Boo-hoo. Worst case scenario, you'll have to find something else to watch for an hour on Thursday nights."

"I don't think you grasp the seriousness of this situation. He's my ideal man. Whoever I marry eventually is going to be the guy who comes closest to matching the version of Dalton Deangelo I have in my mind."

"Then I don't see what the problem is. By going out with the real Dalton, and finding out he's just a regular guy, won't that make it easier for you to find a husband who lives up to your expectations?"

I pointed at her accusingly. "Stop being logical. You're not the logical one in this house. I've seen you talk to cats on the street. You don't just tell them how cute they are, either. You have actual conversations."

She rolled her eyes, then frowned at the jeans I'd flung aside mid-bawl. She bent down and picked them up. "Of course these don't fit you, Peaches. They're mine. I was wondering where these were."

"Don't mess with my head! Are they really yours?"

"They are. Wasn't it obvious when you tried to get them on?"

"How would I know? You're the one who threw out the weigh scale because it had bad feng shui and was making our bathroom depressed or whatever. I thought for sure I'd gained twenty pounds."

"You haven't gained any weight. You're gorgeous. Let's get you dressed before the second act of your pity party."

She started rooting through my closet, setting aside things to try on.

We managed to find my new jeans that were the same color as hers.

"That feels so good," I said, zipping up and fastening the button. "There's no feeling in the world quite like pulling on slightly loose pants. Relaxed clothes are a gift that keeps on giving all day.”

“That’s why I love my old yoga pants,” Nisha said. “The clothing companies know that, so they’re always releasing new colors and new styles. I don’t know what I’d do without my staff discount.”

Nisha worked at a yoga studio that held classes and sold a few lines of clothing, including the locally designed and very comfortable Penntastic brand of sportswear.

The doorbell rang.

I finished buttoning my shirt, and we both ran to the door.

There was no smoldering TV vampire on the porch.

It was a middle-aged man with a brown mustache. He wore a serious expression, like a detective at someone’s door to announce a tragedy.

“I’m Bernard,” he said, offering his hand to shake. “We haven’t been formally introduced. I’m Dalton’s butler.” He had an accent that was similar to Nisha’s. Either he was from England or he had an affectation.

“Butler?” I shook his hand. “Are you messing with me, or are you really a butler? I thought you were his driver, or his bodyguard.”

The solemn man replied, “A butler performs many duties.”

“Is Dalton in the car?”

“Mr. Deangelo is preparing dinner as we speak,” Bernard said. “He sent me to fetch you.”

“Fetch me?”

Nisha, who was standing beside me, grumbled. “A woman is not an item to be fetched.”

“Ladies, I apologize for my choice in words,” Bernard said. “Are you ready to go, Ms. Monroe?”

I turned to Nisha, who shrugged and said, "I guess this is just what famous people with butlers do. They order people delivery like the rest of us order pizza delivery."

I grabbed Nisha's hands. "Come with me."

"I can't come with you," she said sagely. "This is your journey. You must pass through the gauntlet without your wise mentor."

"Finding my jeans doesn't make you a wise mentor," I said.

She squeezed my hands then dropped them as she stepped backward dramatically. "Go now," she said in a spooky voice. "Cross the first threshold. Be brave, young hero."

I grabbed my purse and phone and stepped outside.

Once the door closed, Bernard said, "I had a friend like that in college. If she offers you mushrooms, don't take them."

"Already learned that lesson the hard way," I said.

Bernard chuckled. "Thanks for the wedding cake, Ms. Monroe."

We walked to the car. He opened the back door for me. Before stepping in, I said, "Since we're friends now, Bernard, how about you tell me all of Dalton's dark secrets on the ride?"

He gave me a stony look. "We have a selection of musical playlists available for your listening pleasure," he said.

"You could have just told me your boss doesn't have any dark secrets."

Bernard looked down at his polished black shoes.

"Figured as much," I said as I slid into the back seat.

Chapter 11

Bernard responded to my further attempts to dig up dirt on his boss by turning up the stereo and raising the glass screen separating the back seat from the driver.

We drove past the Cedars, where Dalton and I had attended my cousin's wedding reception, and then on through a large park that was a conservation area for birds and other wildlife. The entire park had been endowed to the city a century ago. It had been untouched by civilization then, except for a couple of access roads, and remained in its natural state. The park included a bog as well as a creek-fed body of water known as Dragonfly Lake.

The park had some walking trails and public features, but no restaurant that I knew of. Its edges were bordered by luxury estates—large properties with hidden mansions designed by famous architects.

I knocked on the glass screen separating me from the driver.

Bernard rolled the divider down and said, "We're almost there."

"Almost where? I thought I was invited for dinner. Is it more of a picnic thing?"

"Mr. Deangelo is cooking for you at his rental property."

"Really? He rented one of these big mansions?"

"Not exactly," Bernard said.

The car rolled through an iron gate, up a driveway, past a mansion, and then into the back, where the property met the preserved woodlands.

The car stopped moving.

I stepped out and saw what Bernard had described as "not exactly" a big mansion.

It was a silver cylinder glinting in the sun. An Airstream camping trailer, sleek and bullet-shaped. The trailer's siding acted as a funhouse mirror, reflecting the surrounding trees and blue sky.

The scent of charcoal briquettes hung in the air.

Dalton Deangelo stood over a barbecue, silver tongs in one hand and a plate of steaks in the other.

The actor waved at Bernard, who got back into the car and drove off.

"This is a surprise," I said. There were birds chirping all around us, and dragonflies flitting around. "We're still in the city, but it's like we're in the country."

"I know. Isn't it great?"

I pointed at the Airstream. "Are you really staying in that little tin can?"

"As long as they let me keep renting it," he said.

"Why not a nice hotel room?"

"Hotel rooms are boring, and they don't have dragonflies." He made some adjustments to the grill. "How do you like your steak?"

"Charred black on the outside and raw in the middle."

He frowned. "Really?"

"That's how my dad makes it."

"But how do you order your steak in a restaurant?"

I laughed. "Have you seen the price of steak in restaurants?"

"Let's try medium-rare," he said.

I came over to stand near the grill. I was glad I'd chosen jeans. Dalton was also wearing jeans, paired with a white shirt that had a waffle-like texture.

Another dragonfly flitted by.

"I used to ride horses around here," I said. "There was a summer camp for girls on the property, years ago."

"Horses, you say? I can make some calls. Bernard's not far away. He can rustle up some horses, if you'd like."

"Not on my account. It's nice just to be here."

The property was right by the lake, and the water was within sight. There was a bird with long legs stalking the shore. "Is that a heron?"

"You're the local. You tell me."

"Oh, definitely a heron." I squinted at the bird. "That's a Knock-Kneed Apple-Jack Heron."

"I think you made that up." He closed the lid on the grill. The meat was still on the plate next to it. "I'm going to let the grill get nice and hot so I can char the outside of your steak the way your dad would."

"Sounds delicious."

He took my hand and grinned at me. "Shall we go for a little wander before dinner? Or can you think of some other way to work up our appetite?"

"A wander sounds perfect."

We set off for a stroll along the lake's shoreline, stopping whenever we found round, flat stones suitable for skipping.

Dalton was really competitive about the stone-skipping, getting excited every time one of his stones went farther than mine, which was pretty much every time, thanks to those muscular arms of his.

We walked past the heron, who was probably wondering why a couple of noisy, pink birds were walking around his lake and throwing perfectly good rocks in the water.

Dalton found a beautiful skipping stone and handed it to me.

I tossed it hard, getting seven good skips before it sank. The sun was moving lower on the horizon, painting a gold streak across the lake.

Dalton picked up a smaller rock and tossed it. His stone skipped so lightly, it seemed to disappear from sight without sinking.

"Crossed the lake with that one," he said, beaming.

"You are the champion."

He reached for my hand and gave it a squeeze, then we turned and headed back to the trailer.

"The Airstream's design is based on aircraft wings." He pointed his chin at the silver trailer, poised gracefully at the edge of the lake. "It's designed for minimal wind resistance, so it hugs the highway, which makes it more stable and also easier on fuel."

"Sounds like you're in love with that trailer. How will you ever leave it after your movie finishes?"

"I don't know. I hope this movie never finishes."

We reached the barbecue, which was hot and ready to cook our steaks.

Dalton said, "Go ahead and have a look inside the trailer if you'd like."

I walked over and opened the screen door, then stepped up into the silver bullet. I thought for sure it was going to rock and make all sorts of creaking noises as I walked through, but it must have been well stabilized for the comfort of rental guests.

The interior looked new, custom, and expensive. To my right, the front of the trailer held a cozy seating banquette, upholstered in red fabric, and a pedestal table. The round table was already set for dinner, complete with fresh flowers. That part of the trailer looked like a photo in a magazine, all pink and red and gorgeous.

The kitchenette looked like a regular high-end kitchen, but in miniature, with the cutest little round sink. Across from the counter and cupboards was more seating, and a built-in desk.

I made my way back to peek at the tiny bathroom, which was small but had everything. The whole trailer was packed with luxury, and nicer than most regular people's homes, despite being a tenth the size.

I peeked into the back area, which was basically just a bed on a platform. At the far end of the bed was a small stack of a dozen books. As a bookstore manager, I considered fifteen books the bare minimum for a bedside stack.

Dalton called in from outside, "Go ahead and pour us some wine while you're in there, will you?"

"Sure, babe!"

He chuckled. "Babe?"

I poured the wine and came to the doorway. "Would you prefer I call you Sir Babe? Seeing as how you were knighted by the Queen of the Undead in season three?"

"Call me whatever you want," he said.

I joined him next to the grill, and we sipped our wine while he worked his magic with the tongs.

"How's this?" He held up a steak with perfect grill marks.

"My dad's are usually more burned, but I'll eat that one. It looks exactly like a steak from a commercial for barbecue sauce."

"It really does," he said. "Should we take a photo for social media?"

"Let's not be those people," I said.

"I agree. Let's not."

He plated both steaks, and we went back into the dining area of the Airstream.

He held up his wine glass. "A toast," he said.

"To what?"

"To enjoying a fine meal in private, without having to photograph it and share it with the world."

I agreed and tapped my glass to his.

He jumped up and grabbed some side dishes from the kitchen, and we dug into our meal.

I had three bites of my steak then asked, "Is this what steak is supposed to taste like? It's so good. I don't miss the charred outside at all."

"I'm glad you like it."

I cut off another piece. "Who's Josie to you?"

He let out an audible breath. "She's someone from my past."

"A friend?"

He glanced up at me, his emerald-green eyes more intense than ever. "Did Josie seem like a friend to you?"

"Not when she was blasting me with my own garden hose. Did you sleep with her?"

"Ew." He shook his head. "It's complicated. But no, I never slept with her."

"But you have slept with a lot of women."

He turned away from me. "Does it matter? None of them are here now."

I looked around the tiny Airstream. "They'd have a hard time hiding inside this place if they were."

"We should check, just to be sure." He set down his utensils and stood.

I set down my utensils as well. "We should?"

"Yes," he said gravely. "We're having a nice evening, and it would be a shame to have it ruined by one of the hundreds of women I've slept with jumping out and frightening us."

"Hundreds?"

He shrugged. "It's more like millions, but I didn't want to scare you."

"Is there anyone you haven't slept with?"

"Remember at the wedding when your mother and I both disappeared for a few minutes?"

My jaw dropped in mock-outrage. "I knew it," I said.

"What can I say? Your mother's my type. Blonde, curvy, falls for my corny lines."

"Just like me."

"Exactly." He turned and walked to the kitchen, where he began systematically opening and closing the cupboards. "I don't see anyone in here."

I squeezed past him and checked the tiny washroom. "Nobody is hiding in here," I reported.

He looked under the built-in desk. "Nobody is lurking down here," he said.

That left only the bedroom.

I walked up to the platform and looked it over. "I don't see anyone," I said.

"Stalkers can be sneaky," he said. "You have to check under the covers."

"Fine." I grabbed one edge and lifted the duvet. "It's just sheets."

"What about at the far end? There's a little space under the table."

I kicked off my shoes and climbed onto the bed. I crawled up to the end and lifted the storage panel. "Empty," I said. "We're all clear." I rolled onto my back. "This is a pretty comfy bed, for a rental."

"Is it?" He kicked off his shoes and climbed up next to me. "I suppose it is," he said.

I rolled to face him. He was facing me, also lying down.

"I'm supposed to be a mermaid," I said.

"You are?" He gave me a confused look. "I'm not sure what game that is."

"It's Dottie's game."

"Is that your aunt who dragged me up to do the chicken dance? I liked her."

"Never mind," I said, and I kissed him.

He kissed me back.

And then...

Fireworks.

Twice.

Fade to black.

Chapter 12

Hours Later

"Dalton?"

The dark-haired actor with the perfect profile murmured and stirred but didn't wake up. While we'd been walking around the lake earlier, he'd mentioned being exhausted from a long day, and he wasn't kidding.

I lay there in the dark, thinking about how I really shouldn't have been there, let alone naked. The walls of the small trailer seemed to be closing in by the minute.

"We forgot to finish dinner," I whispered. "Do you want anything?"

He didn't even stir.

I wriggled my way out of the bed area, feeling like an insect crawling out of a cocoon. I located my clothes and pulled everything on.

I ate some of the dinner we'd abandoned, plus dessert—a very nice panna cotta I located in the fridge.

Dalton continued to sleep.

I tidied up the plates and washed them in the trailer's tiny round sink. Piping-hot water came out of the tap. The Airstream was small, but it had everything.

I kept expecting Dalton to wake from the noises and come out, but he was completely zonked. For the record, I did feel some pride in having worn him out.

After tidying up, I sat in one of the club chairs across from the kitchenette and considered my options.

I could take my clothes back off and climb into the cave of a bed to sleep. But sleeping there would mean eventually using that tiny toilet, on the other side of a paper-thin wall from handsome, perfect Dalton. He probably didn't even go number two, being so perfect. He likely had Bernard, the butler, do it for him.

Staying overnight in the Airstream was not the most appealing option.

It would be better if I left with whatever dignity I had remaining—which wasn't much, considering the wild monkey sounds Dalton had coaxed out of me with his... skills.

I grabbed my purse, combed my hair, and stepped out of the Airstream.

The night air was cool and refreshing.

Now, how was I going to hike out of there? I could go the way I'd come in, but that would mean scaling an iron security gate, only to reach a neighborhood that didn't have bus service.

My best bet was hiking through the woods to the public side of the park. There was a bus loop nearby.

I hiked my purse on my shoulder and took one more look at the Airstream.

It was glowing like a UFO from outer space. Dalton was right about it resembling an airplane minus the wings. How was it glowing? LED lights embedded along some of the aluminum seams? That had to be it.

Or perhaps it was a spaceship in disguise, and Dalton was not a human but an alien sent to earth to test the female earthling's capacity for pleasure. That would explain a lot.

I shivered and forced myself to turn around.

The moon was three-quarters full and at my back as I set off into the dark woods surrounding Dragonfly Lake.

The trail under my feet was mostly smooth, worn flat by many hikers. A few exposed tree roots and fallen branches threatened to trip me up and make me feel even more foolish than I already felt.

Why hadn't I listened to Dottie Simpkins' advice about playing harder to get? The Secret Rules of Love had been a mega bestseller for a reason. If only I'd listened, I could have been in the back seat of a comfortable luxury car, being driven home by Bernard. I could have been looking forward to some far-future date, in which the wild-monkey sounds might have been made at the appropriate point in the relationship.

Instead, I was doing the walk of shame. No. The *hike* of shame. In the dark. With scratchy branches clawing at my bare arms.

The only thing that could make my situation worse would be getting attacked by a sasquatch, or, as the local folks called them, Forest Folk.

The term Forest Folk was misleading, making them sound like sprites or friendly spirits. They were not. Forest Folk were part-human, part-sasquatch cannibals. They ate the toes of children who didn't clean up their bedrooms, and they had Santa Claus on speed dial. Yes, despite being cannibals who lived in the woods, they did have telephones.

The best defense against Forest Folk was the same as what you'd learn in any self-defense course: run away. Forest Folk could regenerate missing body parts almost instantly. Even if you had an ax and chopped off some limbs, they'd just grow new ones and then use their dismembered arms or legs to beat you to death.

A few years back, a librarian gathered up all the local legends and put them in an illustrated story book for children, which she self-published. The book was almost immediately banned, which only increased demand.

As I stumbled through the dark forest, my imagination kicked into overdrive. I regretted all those nights Nisha and I had pored over the banned Forest Folk book at her house as kids, reading by flashlight when we were supposed to be sleeping.

My favorite tale was the one about the Forest Folk man who kidnapped a fair maiden and was transformed by her love back into a human. There was something so romantic about that story, although it did have taboo themes that were likely the cause of the book ban.

I tripped over a root and fell onto my hands, hard. I stumbled up and shook my hands. They were okay. I had to thank all the heavy books I lugged around at Bookworm Books for strengthening my wrists.

Something rustled in the woods.

I froze. The night music—nocturnal insects chirping across the lake—rose up around me.

I whispered, "Hello? Dalton?"

There was a growl from the woods. Did bears growl? Were there bears in the wildlife sanctuary?

My mouth went dry. My heart pounded, but I couldn't move.

"Dalton? Don't joke around. I have a heart condition." That part was a lie. I did not have a heart condition, but the excuse had gotten me out of many unpleasant things such as dodgeball.

The growling came again, and it did not sound like a handsome TV actor playing a prank.

Chapter 13

I told myself the growling creature probably wasn't a bear.

Bears didn't live in the city.

Was it a beaver? Beavers could be aggressive. They could even kill a human if they wanted to.

What wild animal *couldn't* kill a human, if it wanted to? Humans were pretty pathetic without tools.

I slowly pulled my phone from my purse. I turned on the flashlight app and rotated it, illuminating the trees around me.

A pair of eyes glinted back at me.

"Sugar!" I dropped the phone. The light switched off.

Darkness.

Heavy breathing. Mine, plus something else's.

I kneeled and reached for my phone, fumbling around in the dirt and dried leaves.

The other heavy breather was making a lip-smacking sound.

"Forest Folk aren't real," I said to the woods.

The lip-smacking continued.

"You can't eat my toes if I don't believe in you," I said.

More heavy breathing.

I found my phone and started walking again. Fast. The walking turned into jogging.

A male voice called out behind me, "Don't run!"

Don't run? That was exactly what Forest Folk would say right before they caught you. I knew, because it was in the book.

I ran faster.

"Please don't run," the voice pleaded. "It's the worst thing you can do."

"The worst thing I can do is get eaten," I muttered, continuing at my blazing pace of a light jog.

The heavy breathing grew closer.

I felt something at my heels, biting my shoes.

Then there was something nipping at my buttocks.

This caused me to run faster than I had ever run. I may have broken the sound barrier.

But I wasn't fast enough.

Whatever had been pursuing me made its move, hitting me on the back.

I went down, face first. My breath was knocked out of me. I instinctively kept my face down as I covered my neck with my hands in self-defense.

This is it, I thought. *I slept with Dalton Deangelo, and now I'm going to die before I can fully regret it, let alone brag to Nisha about it. Life isn't fair!*

The male voice yelled, "Cujo, heel!"

The beast on my back scrambled off.

I jumped up and whirled around.

There was a man in the woods, and he said, "Peaches!"

I hadn't gotten my breath yet, so I wheezed at him.

The man was Adrian Stromquist. His blond hair was disheveled, and his face was shining with sweat in the moonlight. A skinny German Shepherd sat next to him, panting, its tongue lolling out.

I looked around and gasped, "Where is it? Where's the animal that attacked me?"

"He's right here," Adrian said. "Cujo jumped you. That's why I told you not to run."

I pointed at the dog. "That thing jumped on my back?"

"Barely," Adrian said. "I'm surprised he was able to knock you down." Adrian kneeled next to the dog and said, "Good boy."

"Excuse me? Cujo is a good boy?"

"You were fleeing," Adrian said. "He thought you were a perp. He didn't hurt you, did he?"

"He knocked me down while I was running really fast. I could have broken something."

Adrian smiled his mocking smile. Even in the moonlight, I knew he was loving this opportunity to tease me.

He said, "That was really fast? You were barely moving."

I rubbed my butt. It was wet. "Did he bite me? He bit me!"

"He might have slobbered on you, but he didn't bite you."

"My jeans are wet."

"He's old and toothless. He *gummed* you. That's all. Just a harmless gumming."

"He shouldn't be gumming people, Adrian. Why would you have a crazy dog who gums people and jumps on their backs?"

"He's retired now, but the old police dog training kicks in when he sees people running."

Cujo tilted his head to the side, his big tongue dangling. He was kind of cute. It was hard to stay outraged while looking into the face of a dog who didn't believe he'd done anything wrong.

Adrian said, "He's my dad's dog." Adrian's father was a police officer.

"That's nice," I said through clenched teeth, trying not to scream. "How is your dad?"

"Oh, about the same."

I lost it and started yelling, "Never mind your dad! What are you doing in the woods with a retired police dog, attacking innocent joggers?!"

Adrian came closer, squinting at me in the moonlight. "Are you on drugs?"

"No."

"You seem shaken up," he said.

I crossed my arms. "I thought Forest Folk were going to eat my toes."

He shook his head. "You and Nisha, and your obsession with the supernatural. You always were such silly girls."

"Oh, yeah? If I'm so silly, then why did I just sleep with a vampire?"

Adrian blinked at me. "Whatever drugs you're tripping on, let me know next time you take them." He resumed walking along the trail. "Are you here on your own?"

I nodded. "Long story."

"Fair enough. Want to walk with us back to the parking lot?"

"Can you point me in the direction of the bus loop?"

"Even better. I'll drive you home." He pulled off his jacket and draped it over my shoulders.

The jacket was warm, and appreciated, but I couldn't bring myself to thank him.

We didn't say anything else on the way back to the parking lot.

I got in the passenger seat. Cujo had used up his jumping energy taking me down in the woods, so Adrian gently lifted the elderly dog into the back seat. Adrian lovingly smoothed out the folded towel and patted it for the German Shepherd.

Cujo did three turns while wagging his big, bushy tail in appreciation. He seemed like a nice enough pooch when he wasn't gumming me on my buttocks.

I gave Adrian the address for the house, and he drove us there.

"Nice place," he said, looking it over through the car windows. "That's a new roof with good overhangs. It's just you and Nisha in there?"

"Just the two of us."

"Are either of you dating anyone?"

"She's not. I am. Sort of. I had a date tonight."

Adrian gave me a look of concern. "And he abandoned you in the woods?"

"It's kind of a long story."

"Be careful," Adrian said. "I know you're as tough as ten-dollar nails, but even a girl like you can get hurt."

"A girl like me?"

Adrian took his eyes off me and checked the clock on the dashboard. "Look at the time," he said. "I'd better get home before my parents worry about Cujo."

"What do you mean when you say even *a girl like me* can get hurt?"

"I don't know. You're just so..."

"Fat?"

He pulled his head back and scrunched up his face. "Why do you do that? Why do you put words in people's mouths like that?"

"Why do you have to be so vague and not say what you mean?"

"What were you doing running around in the woods after dark?"

"What were you doing there?"

"Cujo sleeps better when he gets out for a night run."

"So do I."

"Really?"

"I'm going to sleep like a baby tonight." I shoved open the door and stepped out. "Thanks for the ride." I tossed his jacket on the passenger seat. "See you around, Stormy Weather Adrian."

"Don't call me that!"

I slammed the door shut.

Chapter 14

I woke up in my own bed, alone—unless you counted the fig newton cookie crumbs that had spent the night. Judging by the way the crumbs were stuck to my front, they wanted to spend the day with me as well.

I showered off the crumbs, scrubbing off as much of the previous night's shame as I could, then pulled on a cute outfit of dark-brown cords and an olive-green button-down shirt.

In the kitchen, Nisha took one look at me and asked, "Are you off to war this morning, soldier?"

"It's not that bad, is it?"

"You're cuter than that outfit," she said.

"What a fascinating compliment-insult," I said.

"Want some kefir? I made it myself."

I sniffed her bowl of lumpy white stuff. "You made it yourself? Out of what?"

"From whole goat's milk. It's like yogurt."

"No, thanks," I said. "I wouldn't even be in the same room as that goop if you weren't standing in front of the Pop-Tart cupboard." I gestured for her to get out of the way.

We prepared our individual breakfasts and sat at the table together.

Nisha had her long, shiny black hair split into two braids, which she petted while she ate her kefir and granola and judged me. Her supposedly healthy granola had just as much sugar as my breakfast, but I didn't start a fight about it.

She asked, "Are you still upset about last night?"

"What do you think Adrian meant that *a girl like me* could still get hurt?"

"He probably didn't mean anything by it."

"I called him Stormy Weather Adrian. You should have seen the look on his face."

"You two," she said with a head shake. "You'd be perfect for each other, if you could stop resisting it."

"I don't like Adrian. I used to like him, but I don't anymore. I'm an adult now."

"Says the woman eating a Pop-Tart."

"Excuse me. It's called a Toasty Strudel. We can't afford brand-name Pop-Tarts."

"I stand corrected." She chewed on her kefir and granola thoughtfully. "Why are you worried about what Adrian thinks? You just slept with Sir Drake Cheshire. You've got bigger fish to fry."

"Who? Oh, that actor guy." I tossed my head, pretending to have forgotten. "I'll never see him again. You know how those Hollywood types are. Love 'em and leave 'em." I waved my toasted strudel, dropping crumbs. "He's probably sending his butler out for someone different tonight. He had a blonde last night, so maybe tonight will be a redhead."

"Don't sell yourself short. Actors date regular people sometimes." She sighed. "Why am I wasting my energy? You're so paranoid about rejection that you run away from guys before they can reject you."

"Oh, yeah? What about you? You're in love with your boss."

She frowned. "I'm not in love with him. Besides, even if I was, he only dates white girls with tiny boobs."

"Your boobs aren't *that* big, Nisha."

She rolled her eyes. "Fair enough. I insult-complimented you first."

I sighed. "We always want what we can't have."

"Do you want Dalton Deangelo?"

"I know I can't have him," I said. "Therefore, yes."

"If you could have him, would you stop wanting him?"

"I don't know."

"Close your eyes and visualize having him. It's your wedding day. How do you feel?"

I got up from the table and pushed in my chair. "It is way too early in the morning for you to be probing my soul."

"Well, meditate on it," she said. "We got some new yoga mats in at the studio, so I might not be home for dinner. We can resume soul-probing tomorrow."

"Yes, dear." I kissed her on top of her head and left for work.

I walked outside, where I was greeted by Mr. Galloway. My retired neighbor was out in his front yard, tending his roses.

He said, "That was quite the ruckus on your lawn on Saturday night."

"We're the only rental house on the block, Mr. Galloway. Someone has to play the role of neighborhood riffraff."

He chuckled. "You girls are all right. Not like the last tenants Doug had in there." He handed me a rose. "Take this with you to your bookstore," he said.

"It's not my bookstore, Mr. Galloway. It belongs to the Olivier family, along with half the real estate on the block. Gordon Olivier runs the store now, when he's not in Arizona with his Canadian girlfriend, Ida, who, from what I hear, is a terrible cook."

"I know Gordon Olivier. I never see him there."

"Gordon likes money, but he's never been into books. Also, he's not that great with money. He keeps doing useless things, like signing up for those internet coupon deals that only lose money.”

“Is that so?” Mr. Galloway handed me more roses for my bouquet.

“He wants to turn the store into a wine boutique and move the books across the street to a smaller storefront the family owns.”

Mr. Galloway’s face lit up. “A wine boutique? We could use one of those in the neighborhood.”

“Traitor,” I said.

Mr. Galloway handed me a few more roses and sent me on my way.

I walked down to Baker Street then up to Bookworm Books.

My cousin, Megan Gardenia, was standing in front of the bookstore with a bouquet of roses. Megan and her sister, Tina, who’d gotten married on Saturday, ran Gardenia Flowers, also on Baker Street.

Megan looked at my handful of Mr. Galloway’s roses and said, “Someone’s been putting out lately.”

Megan Gardenia was anything but subtle. Some people said bluntness ran in our family. I liked to think I was more gracious with Megan, who had, until recently, gone by the nickname Meenie for good reason.

“These roses are from my neighbor,” I said.

She raised an eyebrow. “You’re knocking boots with your neighbor?”

“He’s in his seventies.”

“Be careful on his old-man ticker,” she said. “A man that age can’t handle the reverse cowgirl.”

“I’ll keep that in mind. How’s the dentist?”

“He’s in tears daily because you need to come in for that root canal. Don’t be such a chicken.”

I unlocked the door to the bookstore but didn't push it open yet. "Who are those flowers for?"

Megan grinned. "They're for you, Peaches. Some guy with an accent ordered them by phone. Obviously it was Dalton Deangelo doing a character voice, but he did have me going for a minute."

"Dalton sent me flowers?"

"You're so lucky," Megan said. "I had to wait until I was basically an old maid before I found a guy who could handle all of this." She waved at her body in general. "You're only twenty-two, Peaches, and you've already caught yourself an A-lister." She punched me on the shoulder. Hard. "Lucky duck."

"Thanks, but I'm not sure I've caught anyone." I sniffed the loose roses in my hand. "Plus I'm not ready to give up what I have with Mr. Galloway. He's reliable, and he's always home in bed by nine o'clock. Actors are... less reliable."

"Until you marry them and housebreak them," Megan said. "I call dibs on bridesmaid duties."

She handed me the bouquet then gave me a cute, scrunched-face smile before turning and jogging away, back to her flower shop.

I pushed open the door, my hands full of two bouquets of roses.

Chapter 15

My first customer of the day was Bernard, the butler.

In his posh accent, he said, "You disappeared on us last night, Ms. Monroe. I was supposed to see to your safe return home."

I held out my hands. "As you can see, I'm in one piece."

"So it would seem. Very well. Mr. Deangelo requests your company tonight, if you can make yourself available."

"Tonight?" Dottie Simpkins would have scolded me for even *considering* making a same-day date. But Dottie Simpkins wasn't there. I asked, "What does your boss have in mind?"

Frowning under his bushy, ultra-serious mustache, Bernard said, "That's confidential."

"Ooh. A mystery. How dramatic. Is your boss always so dramatic?"

"Yes."

"Bernard," I said. "It's just me. I'm a regular girl. It's just us here. Two people who like cake. Am I right?"

"I do like cake," he admitted.

"I'd like to know what I'm agreeing to before I say yes. Wouldn't you?"

He gave me a hint of a smile below his bushy mustache. "I don't know what his plans are, exactly, but I did make reservations nearby for dinner." He winked.

"Gotcha." I winked right back.

He looked at the Gardenia Flowers bouquet on the counter. "I see you received the bouquet." He glanced over at the other bouquet, from Mr. Galloway, and frowned. "Another suitor?"

"As a matter of fact, yes," I said. "All the eligible bachelors have been coming around, trying to get a handful of my peaches."

"So it would seem." He gave me a curious look. "How did you get home last night? I was parked by the gate, and I didn't see anyone come by."

"I'm very sneaky under the cover of night. Like a ninja."

Bernard nodded. "So it would seem," he said again.

"I'll tell you the secret of how I ninja-jumped my way out of there without detection, but you have to tell me a secret in return. One about your boss."

"As for your ninja skills, let's leave it to the imagination," he said. "Did you read the card?"

"Not yet." I'd forgotten about the card that came with the bouquet. I pulled it out of the small envelope and read it out loud. "*Thanks for the fun.*"

"Indeed," Bernard said, sounding very butler-like.

"*Thanks for the fun*? What's that supposed to mean?"

"I suppose it means that Mr. Deangelo enjoyed your company."

"He didn't need to send me a note about that. I could tell he was enjoying my company, Bernard. Either that or he's an amazing actor." I tapped my chin. "But I don't think he was acting. Some things you can't fake if you're a guy."

Bernard blinked. His face reddened. "Indeed."

"What restaurant did your boss have you make a reservation at for this mysterious date tonight?"

"I cannot say."

"Well, I cannot say if I'm available, so put me down as a maybe."

"A maybe?" Bernard did not look pleased. I guessed that most of the girls he was sent out to fetch for his boss were more eager.

I asked, "Is there anything else I can help you with since you're already here? A book, perhaps? You must spend a lot of time sitting in your boss's car with nothing to do."

Bernard glanced around the shop. "Perhaps you could tell me what single people in this city do for fun."

"The usual stuff. Hang out with friends."

"But how does one make friends? Everyone tells me a place like this is much friendlier than Los Angeles, but that has not been my experience."

"Oh, Bernard. You can't just roll into town and expect people to show up at your door with pie. You need to make the first move. Take an interest. Why don't you check out our community cork board over there and find something you're interested in?" I pointed him in the direction of the corkboard, which was covered in five layers of colored papers promoting all sorts of local events.

He started looking through the offerings, his hands folded behind his back.

After a moment, he carefully extracted one tear-tab for a community event, and then another.

"That's the spirit," I said. "Rip those tear-tabs. That's what they're for."

The bells on the front door jingled. Another person came in.

Bernard stuffed the tiny papers into his suit jacket, gave me a businesslike nod, and left.

The person coming in was my father, a slim, middle-aged man with ginger hair. He gave the butler, who was dressed in an old-fashioned suit, a curious look.

"Odd fellow," my dad commented after the door had closed.

"You're one to talk," I said. "They don't get odder than you."

"He didn't leave with any books. What was he doing here? He wasn't bothering you, was he?"

"Dad! Don't worry about it. People come in to browse. It's not against the law. We're doing fine, and sales are steady."

My father had already moved on to other concerns, mainly electrical. He leaned over to inspect the window display then frowned up at the halogen spotlights. "If you retrofit some LEDs in there, it won't heat up and fade the book covers so much."

"Then what will be my incentive to change the window display?"

He stared at me like he couldn't believe we shared DNA.

The ventilation system whirred on, bringing in donut smells from next door, as usual.

My father tipped his head to the side. "Is that the air conditioning? You could simply open the front door for a bit. You should air the place out at night, get it good and cold, then pull the blinds until you get here in the morning."

"Dad, it's not my bookstore. I get paid the same no matter what the electricity bill is."

He scratched his head, looking like a classic absent-minded professor. My father ran a niche business selling parts for radio-control helicopters, or as we liked to call them, "flying chainsaws." He rented office space above one of the Baker Street stores, so it wasn't unusual to have him pop in on a weekday.

"Your mother sent me," he said. "She wants you to bring your new actor boyfriend to dinner on

Friday. She hardly got to talk to him at your cousin's wedding."

"You mean she didn't get a chance to grill him about his intentions."

He gave me a perplexed look. "Is that not the sort of thing a parent should be concerned about?"

"Dalton's not even my boyfriend," I said. "We've only had two dates, including the wedding. It's not serious."

My father examined the lavish flower bouquet on the counter. "Flowers," he said. "From him?"

"Yes."

"Flowers are serious. This is a serious bouquet. Even if your cousin gave him a family discount, that's a pricey arrangement."

"He's rich," I said. "He probably spends more on one pair of underwear than you paid for that suit."

My father blinked. "Tell me you haven't seen his underwear."

"I haven't," I said. Only because it had been dark under the covers. "Anyway, rich people aren't like us. Dalton has a butler. You know that serious man with the mustache who was leaving when you got here? That's Bernard. He's the butler."

"I'd like a butler," my father said, as casually as if he'd been commenting on his desire for a grilled cheese sandwich.

"What I mean is, he's a famous actor, and I'm a chubby girl who manages a bookstore. Honestly, what do you think is going to happen between us?"

My father grimaced then looked up at the lighting over the counter. "You should replace that whole fixture. I've got an extra one I can bring by."

It was such a Peter thing—my father's name was Peter—to evade a difficult subject and obsess over something involving electricity instead.

"Sure, Dad," I said. "Bring over the new light fixture anytime."

"What shall I tell your mother about dinner on Friday?"

"It's only Tuesday today. A lot has happened in the last few days. I have no idea what will be going on by the end of the week."

"What shall I tell her? You know how your mother is."

"Tell her I'll see what I can do."

"She's making ham," he said, and then he left.

Chapter 16

My father came by with a new light fixture in the afternoon. He'd taught me how to do basic electrical stuff, so I stayed in the store after closing and installed it.

The phone rang. We were closed, but I answered anyway.

"Good evening, Bookworm Books."

A flirtatious man replied, "Is it a good evening?"

"That depends on who this is and why you're calling."

"You hurt poor Bernard's feelings when you didn't say yes to dinner."

I smiled and wrapped the long, curly phone cord around my hand. "Poor Bernard," I said. "I hope you're paying him extra for all the errands you make him do."

"He's well taken care of."

"Sounds to me like he's the one who does all the care-taking. Does he iron your underpants?"

"Yes, and he uses too much starch."

"I knew it."

"Are you hungry?"

"No." My stomach growled. "Yes."

"Is this Niro's place across from you any good? I'm standing out front, reading the menu. It's so colorful. They have a Forest Folk platter that's free if you eat the whole thing, but I don't know if I'm that hungry. Also, I need a local to explain to me what Forest Folk are. In the illustration, they look like sasquatches."

"You're at Niro's?"

"You tell me."

Niro's was across the street from the bookstore. I went to the front window and looked. There was a handsome, dark-haired man standing across the street, waving at me.

"I see you," I said. "It's funny. You look like a regular person at this distance."

"Thanks, I think. What's the deal with this Niro's place? Any connection to Robert De Niro, the actor?"

"Zero connection. It's not even that Italian."

"What are you doing over there? Aren't you closed?"

"I was doing important manager stuff. I changed a light fixture. You'd be so proud of me. I used the ladder instead of standing on a chair."

"So you can keep promises," he said. "Good to know."

"I was extremely safety conscious the whole time."

"Why don't you lock up that bookstore and come join me for a carb-heavy meal that my personal trainer will slap me senseless for eating?"

"Niro's has some tasty salads."

"Salads? Forget salads!" He held the phone away from his ear and gave me what I assumed was a dirty look from across the street. "Who is this? I want the naughty Peaches. The one who's a bad influence on me."

"Give me two minutes to lock up."

"Two minutes. I'm starting the timer. If you go over the time limit, there will be Penalty Minutes."

"What?"

"Penalty Minutes. Tick, tick. Time's running out."

I unwound myself from the phone cord, then hung up the phone and raced around in a panic. Penalty Minutes? I didn't want to rack up Penalty Minutes, whatever they were.

My finger was shaking as I punched in the alarm code, 1225. The owner chose that number because it was the date of the only day the store was closed.

I ran out the front door, then back in for my purse, then back out again, my heart pounding as the countdown on the alarm beeped down.

I was worried about Dalton's Penalty Minutes, which would pile up fast if I set off the alarm and had to deal with the security company.

When I reached the other side of the street, Dalton said, "Three seconds to spare. Nice work."

"Why do I feel like you tricked me?"

"Because I did," he said.

"That must be why."

As we stood there, a couple walked out of the restaurant. The woman stopped in her tracks and stared at Dalton. "You're him, aren't you?" To her husband, she said, "It's Drake. The vampire. I heard he was shooting a movie here."

The husband said, "I don't think that's him."

"It is," the woman said, as though Dalton wasn't standing right there in person.

"He's too tanned," the husband said. "Plus look at his perfect teeth."

The wife said, "The teeth on the show are prosthetics. It's him. Those are his regular teeth."

Dalton gave me a tired look, then suddenly snapped into action. He pulled me in front of him, making a horrible snarling sound as he bit me on the neck. It was not a gummy bite, like I'd gotten from Cujo in the woods the night before, but an honest-to-goodness bite with teeth.

I squealed and said, "Ooh, Bitey!"

The woman stared at us with a mix of horror and adulation on her face. The husband got out his phone.

"I need a picture of this," he said. "Mind if my wife gets in there?"

"Sure," Dalton said, then he pretended to bite the man's wife on the neck. I pretended to not be jealous. His lips got a little closer to her skin that I would have liked to have seen.

The husband said to Dalton, "Give the ol' gal a good bite. Really go for it."

Dalton waggled his eyebrows and said, "I'm afraid if I do, she'll never be the same."

The woman nearly collapsed in a heap of giggles and lust. He lunged at her neck anyway. She screamed.

The husband managed to take the photo, which was good for both of them and their safety. If Dalton had pretend-bitten the woman's neck a bit longer, I might have staged some drama of my own. I didn't like sharing my toys.

The couple finally walked away and left us alone.

I said to the actor, "You seem to enjoy interacting with your fans."

He gave me a saucy look. "Jealous? Don't be. I only have eyes for one fan."

"Me?"

"I'm not sure. She only joined my fan club recently. Her screen name is Peach-a-licious."

"You know I joined your fan club? I'll just die now." I bowed my head and turned. "Please excuse me while I die."

"Don't be embarrassed. I only log in once in a while. When I saw your name, it made me happy."

"Good. That's the only reason I did it. Not to get access to all the fanfiction. Have you read any of that stuff? You've got some weird fans out there."

"I try not to. Especially the stories where I'm having a romantic relationship with... Connor." He made a yuck face.

"Ew. Connor is the worst."

Dalton stepped closer and seized me in his arms. "Kiss me," he said.

We were out in the open, and I felt self-conscious, so I gave him a timid peck on the lips.

"No," he said, giving me a smoldering look. "Kiss me like I'm dangerous. Kiss me like I'm bad for you."

His dark hair flopped around in a breeze, ruffling on his forehead above his dreamy, too-cute eyes.

Oh, he was dangerous. And bad for me.

I stood up on tiptoes and gave him a real kiss. The smell of his skin felt more familiar than it should have. His hands on my back felt like they belonged there. The evening sun was glinting off the windows and vehicles around us. His hands dropped to the place Cujo had gummed me. He grabbed hold and pulled me against his body.

I resisted and tore myself away.

He gazed down at me affectionately. "You nailed it," he said. "I told you to kiss me like I was dangerous and bad for you, and you nailed it. It would be amazing to direct you. Have you considered acting?"

"I wasn't acting," I said. "You are dangerous. And you are bad for me."

He raised an eyebrow. "Is this because I fell asleep last night? I didn't mean to be so rude. When I woke up and you were gone, I thought maybe I'd dreamed the whole thing."

"Oh, I'm real."

He grinned. "You sure are." He pulled me toward the restaurant's door. "Let's discuss how real you are over some food and wine, like civilized adults."

"Speak for yourself."

"You don't like food and wine?"

"I'm not a civilized adult."

He gave me a confused head shake and pulled me into the restaurant anyway.

Chapter 17

Our waiter at Niro's was a man who'd waited on me and my family many times over the years.

"Edward!" I jumped up and hugged him. "You look so handsome dressed up like this." He was wearing black pants and a crisp white shirt.

He gave me a bashful look. "It's a big upgrade from the rodent costume, wouldn't you say?"

"Where *is* the rodent costume?"

"We gave it a dignified burial," he said solemnly.

I slid back into my seat and explained to Dalton, "This place used to be called Chunky Cheese. It was a knockoff Chuck E. Cheese, and my absolute favorite restaurant. My family came here every year for my birthday."

Edward said to my date, "The decor was different. And the lighting was much brighter back then."

"It's so dark in here now," I said to the waiter. "How are things going with the new owners?"

"Fine so far," Edward said. "Even after all this time, there are still a few typos on the menu, so I apologize in advance for that, but the food is terrific."

"It smells amazing," I said. "And the place looks busy."

Edward glanced around with obvious pride. "We're past the one-year mark and still building up clientele. Speaking of anniversaries, I must have been off work on your last birthday, Peaches."

I ducked my head in shame. "I went somewhere else for my twenty-second." I straightened up right away. "But it won't happen again. I'll be back here for the next one, even though the place is so different now. Will you sing the song?"

"It won't be the same without the rodent costume, but I'll do it for you." He put his hands behind his back and asked if we had any questions about the menu.

Dalton said, "No, but I have so *many* questions that aren't about the menu. Are there photos of you in this rodent costume? What kind of rodent was it?"

"For legal reasons, it was definitely not a rat," Edward said, winking. "There are framed photos in the hallway leading to the restrooms."

Dalton looked at me, his emerald-green eyes twinkling. "I love this place. I love this street. I love this whole city."

Edward said, "Wait 'til you try the garlic bread. I'll bring a basket right over."

Dalton laughed, then stopped. "Oh, right," he said, as though talking to himself. "People still eat bread."

Edward tilted his head. "Are you not from around here, sir?"

"He's a famous Hollywood actor," I said. "He plays Drake Cheshire on *One Vamp to Love*."

Dalton frowned at me. "Are you showing me off?"

"Edward's practically family," I explained.

"Good casting," Edward said, nodding as he looked over the actor. "I can picture you biting a lot of necks." He suddenly looked horrified. "You'd better not be biting our Peaches." He came around behind my chair and put his hands on my shoulders protectively.

"Too late," I said. "The horses have been let out of the barn."

"Oh, dear," Edward said, then he excused himself to get us our garlic bread.

I looked over the menu and said, "I think I'll have the third item down. I believe it is pronounced *spaghetti*."

"I've heard of that," Dalton said. "Is it Italian?"

"Yes. It's actually named after the tree that grows the noodles, the Spaghettini Opulus."

"Is that so?"

"You really *must* see the orchards at harvest time. They're magnificent."

Dalton raised an eyebrow. "You're very cultured for someone who isn't even a civilized adult."

"Thank you." I returned my attention to my menu. "I just need to decide how many balls I want."

"Pardon me?"

I explained, "The spaghetti and balls comes with any number of balls."

Dalton squinted and held up his menu to the dim light. "Spaghetti and balls," he said. "Must be a typo."

I stuck my nose in the air. "I have no idea what you're talking about. All the cultured people enjoy spaghetti and balls."

"Interesting," he said. "What is the usual number of balls for you?"

"I can handle two balls at a time for sure."

"I bet you can."

"But I'm willing to juggle three or more," I said.

"If I find myself with too many balls, you could help with some of mine."

"I'd be happy to help with your balls, if you're not man enough to handle them on your own."

"Oh, I can handle multiple balls just fine on my own," he said. "Sometimes it's nice to share your balls."

"It's nice to have someone to share your balls with," I replied.

Edward returned with the garlic bread. Dalton's nostrils flared visibly.

We ordered our meals, plus an appetizer and a bottle of wine.

Dalton dug into the garlic bread. "Do not tell my trainer," he said gravely as he lifted a steaming, buttery slice to his mouth.

"It can be our little secret, but only if you make sexy noises while you eat the carbs."

"Mmm," he said. "You little minx."

"Are you talking to me or the bread?"

"Bit of both," he said around his mouthful. "Why did you leave last night?"

"I like the Airstream, but it's not really my style."

"What is your style? Do you want to get a hotel room tonight?"

I gave him an indignant look. He was making assumptions. This was exactly why Dottie Simpkins, co-author of *The Secret Rules of Love*, advised women not to accept a date without three days' notice.

I replied, "What makes you think I would be going anywhere with you after dinner?"

"Someone has to help me burn off these carbs," he said.

I gave him a mock wounded expression. "Is that all I am to you?"

"Of course not," he said. "You're research."

I tore off a piece of the bread for myself. "It's a good thing the bread is nonstop, or I wouldn't get any." I took a small bite. "What do you mean, I'm research?"

He looked away. "Oh, uh, it's just something actors say. It doesn't mean anything."

"That's the second time you've said it, though."

"It is? Huh." He stuffed a huge chunk of garlic bread in his mouth and pretended to be unable to speak coherently.

"Tell me about this independent film you're shooting this summer."

He stuffed more bread in his mouth and gave me a helpless look.

"Order another basket when Edward comes by," I said as I got to my feet. "I just need to visit the ladies' room."

He muttered incoherently.

"You're not low-carb," I said. "You're a carb disposal unit."

He kept eating.

I went to the ladies' room, where I freshened up.

I also made a very important phone call to Nisha.

When I returned to the table, there was more garlic bread. Dalton pretended to not notice me there as he spoke dirty talk to the garlic bread. Then he pretended to be embarrassed over getting caught.

"You're as bad as my roommate," I said. "She talks that way to neighborhood cats."

"I like cats," he said.

"That's a random fact," I replied.

"Some people don't like cats," he said. "Controlling people, usually. They don't like cats because cats refuse to be told what to do." He grinned. "Like you."

"That must be why you like me."

He looked me in the eyes. "I do like you."

"You're high on garlic bread."

"I am," he said.

"Aren't you afraid of getting fat like me?"

He frowned. "You're not fat."

"It's dark in here, and I'm wearing dark clothes. Plus you're so high on garlic bread you can't even see straight."

He kept frowning. "I just want to be happy," he said. "This garlic bread makes me happy. So do you."

"If my best friend, Nisha, were here right now, she'd lecture you on the vast differences between hedonistic pleasure and actual happiness."

"Aren't those the same?"

"Nisha says the problem with the modern world is people think pleasure and happiness are the same thing when they aren't."

"She sounds wise."

"She is, for twenty-two."

He licked some garlic butter off his thumb. "I wonder what your best friend would say about this movie I'm doing. I'm scared about the damage it could do to me."

"You're doing your own stunts?"

He poured some wine evenly between our glasses, looking very serious and sad.

"The damage is emotional, or psychological, I guess. Have you done any acting?"

"Sometimes at the bookstore," I said. "I act like I'm not bored senseless when I am."

"Imagine acting like you've just walked away from a horrific car accident, and your small child didn't survive."

I imagined Elliot being hurt, and the pain was so strong, it manifested as physical pain in my guts.

"That's horrible," I said, shaking my head. "Don't say stuff like that or you'll give me nightmares."

"That's what acting is like. You can't avoid the darkness. You have to embrace it to deliver a believable appearance. If you aren't suffering, the audience won't connect."

"Can't you just say the words and pretend?"

"That's pretty much all you can do. Sounds simple enough, except there's a part of your brain that doesn't know it's pretend. Your ears hear the words in your voice, and you believe it. Your soul believes it."

I frowned and played with the silverware before me.

"You seem to be having fun, though. As Drake, the vampire. You're always grinning and having a blast."

"True. The TV show is a lot of fun. And last summer's straight-to-digital movie that I filmed here was light and fluffy. But the movie I'm doing this summer is different." He paused dramatically. "It wears on me."

I nodded. "Sucky." I picked up my wine. "No pun intended, Sir Drake, but that sounds sucky."

His expression went from vampiric brooding to amusement. "It *is* sucky. That's the perfect word." He sat up straight, looking more vital than ever. "I love how you put things in perspective. You have a real gift for stating the obvious, exactly when I need to hear it. Embracing a dark role is sucky. But it's also a challenge, and it's what I desperately wanted, so why am I complaining?"

I shrugged. "People have to complain about something."

"Do they?"

We were interrupted by a skinny blonde approaching the table. She squeezed my shoulder and said, "Peaches?"

I looked up at her. "Brittany Brown?"

She grinned, deepening the adorable dimples in her cheeks. I hadn't seen Brittany Brown since high school, but the warm feelings rushed back. She was one of those girls everybody liked. I might have hung out with her more if she hadn't been best friends with a drama queen, Sunshine Banks.

"It's me," the always-perky little blonde said, pressing her fingertips to her dimples. "I'm surprised you recognized me with these puffy eyes." She sniffed, looking pitiful. "I've just been cryin' over a guy. An older man." She waved a hand. "It's over. The past is the past. It's great to see you. Why have we fallen out of touch?"

"Life," I said. "I don't know."

"We used to have so much fun together, all of us girls."

"We should hang out sometime," I said.

She gasped. "That would be *amazeballs*!"

"I'm renting a house with Nisha. We've been talking about having a party."

Brittany's pretty blue eyes widened. A huge smile spread across her face. "*Awesomesauce!* We can invite Sunshine and get the whole gang back together!"

Ugh, Sunshine. Also known as Little Miss Guess What. Everything was a big production, a big secret with an elaborate teaser campaign. Whenever you finally found out the actual "big" news, it was wildly disproportionate to the amount of fuss Sunshine put into it. Plus there was the whole thing with her aspirations of becoming a famous singer.

"Sounds great," I lied.

I glanced over at Dalton, who was watching our exchange with an amused expression.

I started to introduce Brittany to him, but she interrupted me.

Brittany asked, in her usual breathless-plus-bubbly voice, "Did you hear Adrian Stromquist is back in town?"

"Yes," I said. "He's flat broke and living with his parents. It's tragic, but inevitable. Stormy Weather Adrian brings his raincloud of doom with him wherever he goes."

"That's too bad," she said, jiggling and standing on one foot, kicking the other up behind her. Double-wow. I'd completely forgotten about that kick. Why didn't I have a signature move? I had to work on that.

"He'll be fine," I said. What was that expression he'd used to describe me? "He's as tough as ten-dollar nails."

"And cuter than ever," she said. She kicked again then said, "I have to get back to my table. My dad got a promotion, so we're celebrating. I'll have to meet your friend later." She winked at Dalton, then backed away while squealing, "Byeeee!"

Dalton and I replied in unison, "Byeeee!"

I looked down at my drab brown cords and green shirt. "If I'd known it was date night plus high school reunion, I would have dressed up."

"You look perfect."

"Maybe when I finally become a civilized adult, I won't care what other people think of me."

"Civilized adults still care what people think of them. Maybe more than when they were kids."

I shook my fist in mock rage. "My parents lied to me!"

He pursed his lips. "All parents lie. The good ones tell comforting lies."

"Dark. Next you'll be quoting Nietzsche."

"Not without a script in front of me, I won't." He gave me a sly grin.

Edward arrived with our dinner.

We ate the spaghetti and continued to tease each other about the meatballs, among other things.

My best friend and guardian angel for the evening, Nisha Patel, arrived just in time for dessert, which was tiramisu.

"What a coincidence, bumping into you here," Nisha said, hitting her dialog a bit hard.

"Join us," I said, shifting over on the bench seat.

I introduced Dalton to my best friend and roommate.

"This is brilliant," Nisha said as she settled in, her British accent increasing with her excitement. "Just brilliant."

Dalton beamed at her.

She gave him a squint then said, "You're not short in real life. People always say how small actors are, but you're full-size."

Dalton gave me a wide-eyed look and pressed his lips together tightly.

Nisha saw the look and said, "What? Have I offended you? I'm bloody sorry if I did."

"That's not it," I said. "He wants to make a double-entendre based on what you said. Probably something about being full-size where it counts?"

Dalton nodded vehemently.

Nisha put her arm across me protectively. "It sounds like I got here just in time." She shook her finger at Dalton. "You behave yourself, young man. I'll be chaperoning the rest of the evening."

And she did.

Which was why I finished the date with my clothes on, like a good soldier in the war of love.

Chapter 18

After Nisha and I gave Dalton a hug and a kiss goodnight—she gave the hug and I gave the kiss—my roommate and I walked back to the house. Dalton had offered to have Bernard drive us, but home wasn't far from Baker Street. Plus Nisha believed strongly in walking after dinner to aid in digestion, or, as she put it, "flow of *ama*." I had a suspicion the post-dinner walks had something to do with the volume of lentils she ate, and her need to empty the gas chambers.

I made sure the handsome actor wasn't following us, or having his butler follow us, and said, "Well?"

After a moment, Nisha spoke slowly in her charming English accent. "He's not the bloke I thought he would be."

"Because he's tall?"

"Not that. I didn't think he'd be so *sensitive*. All that talk about the psychological distress of acting, I wasn't expecting that. He's a sensitive guy. He pretends to be calm on the surface, but he's just good at hiding how anxious he is."

"You've seen the show. He's constantly running around shirtless and emotional. How much more sensitive can you get?"

"But that's acting, and it's always over the top. His character gets worked up weekly over whatever it is the Queen of the Undead is making him do. The way he was back there at Niro's was different. He was sensitive in a real way, which is nice, for a man."

"But? I hear a *but* in there."

"But I think he has anxiety. It might come from past trauma causing spiritual blockages."

"Nobody's perfect."

"I'm not criticizing him, Peaches."

"I hear another *but*."

"But I'm worried about the effect he has on you. I don't mind that you called me to chaperone you home from the date, but I'm a wee bit concerned that you felt you had to."

"I didn't *feel* I had to, Nisha. I *had to*. He started talking about getting a hotel room. I knew I wasn't going to be able to resist, so I did the smart thing. I immediately ran to the bathroom and called you to save me."

"Rather than telling him no," she said.

"I didn't want to ruin the mood."

"Was it that, or are you truly unable to resist him?"

"I'm like Oscar Wilde. I can resist anything but temptation."

"There's a group for sex and love addiction at the community center."

"Nisha!" My exasperation showed in my voice. "I called you one time for help out of a tricky spot, and you got a tasty dessert out of it. I don't think we're at the point where I need to be tied up in a straitjacket and committed to the love asylum."

"It's not the first time you've needed me to rescue you," she said. "There was the guy with the shaved head, and the delivery guy, and that poor kid who just wanted to mow our lawn."

"Oh, pssh." I waved a hand. "The gardener was no kid. He was over eighteen. So what if I invited him in to mow my lawn and he freaked out?"

"I'm just saying there's a pattern. It's more detectable from the outside."

"What are you saying? Are you telling me I'm some sort of sex addict?"

"I'm asking if you think you are."

"Nope." I crossed my arms and walked faster. "I'm young, and I want to have a little fun before I'm old and married. I'm not like you. I'm not content to read self-help books at home on Saturday night while pining after the same guy for years."

She took a moment to chew it over then said, "That's fair. I suppose I had that coming. You're right about us being young, though. It's okay that we don't have everything figured out."

"Good," I said.

"Good," she agreed.

We rounded a corner and headed toward the park.

"I saw Brittany Brown at the restaurant before you got there," I said. "She was her usual cheerleader self, kicking up her foot and everything. I didn't get to introduce her to Dalton because she started pouring her heart out about her own messed-up love life. She said her eyes were puffy because she'd been crying over some older guy."

Nisha stopped walking. "I knew it," she said.

I stopped as well. "You knew what?"

"That's who Noah was dating. Brittany Brown."

"You never told me that."

"Because you roll your eyes whenever I talk about him. You roll your eyes and tell me to get a life."

"Noah was dating Brittany? I thought he preferred skinny blondes who were more angsty and messed up. Limp little abandoned princesses that he could rescue. Brittany comes from a nice family, and she's happy."

"That's probably why it didn't work out," Nisha said. "I thought I sensed a change in his energy. This explains everything. They broke up."

"Now he's free to date you, Nisha. Lucky girl. How's your abandoned-princess game? Can you look wan and needy?"

She sighed.

I said, "Who's the sex and love addict now?"

She sighed again.

We got walking again. We reached the dog park and stopped to watch the happy critters cavorting around on the grass.

One of the dogs jumped on top of another one, knocking its legs out from underneath it.

Nisha laughed out loud. She turned to me and said, "Do you remember Lionheart?"

"Was that one of your stuffed animals?"

"It was the pony my parents rented for my birthday party the first year we moved here. Do you remember that party?"

I crossed my arms. "Vaguely," I said, which was a lie.

"You were so mad when they wouldn't let you ride Lionheart," Nisha said. "Then you went crazy and dumped cupcakes down the trainer's shirt."

"Excuse me? I went crazy? No way. That trainer had it coming. It was so rude of him to take one look at me and say I was too fat to ride the pony."

"He didn't say that. He said you were too *mature*, and he offered to let you ride the adults' horse."

My arms remained crossed. "It wasn't even a horse. It was a mule. I didn't want to get on that smelly old thing. Not while you and Brittany and Sunshine rode around on Lionheart, the cute pony, gloating all over the place."

"You could have gotten on the weigh scale. That was all the trainer asked."

"Step on a scale in front of everyone else? No way."

"The rest of us did. Sunshine was tall already, and she barely made the weight limit. You were probably within range."

I fought back tears as the memory of that humiliating day hit me hard.

"Why are you even bringing this up, Nisha?"

She shrugged. "Just making conversation. Aren't you happy I'm not moaning about Noah right now?"

"Sure, but why did you have to bring up Lionheart? Are you trying to make me feel bad? Are you that jealous that I might have something going on with a guy who's actually into me, as opposed to your unattainable, perfect Noah?"

Nisha gave me a shocked look.

"He's never going to date you," I said. "I hope you know that. So what if he's broken up with Brittany? It's never going to happen between you two."

Nisha's jaw dropped.

Even the dogs in the dog park were staring at us.

I started marching toward the house.

"Peaches," my best friend called after me. "I didn't mean anything by it."

"That's not true." I turned around and walked away backward while giving her the stink-eye. "You're the one who says people don't bring things up by coincidence. You dug up that story because you wanted to put me in my place. You wanted to remind me that I'm the screw-up who pitches a tantrum and throws cupcakes at people."

She held up both hands. "Nobody's perfect," she said.

I snorted, turned around, and marched home like I had Cujo nipping at my heels.

Chapter 19

I skipped breakfast at home because I hadn't apologized to Nisha for flipping out at her, and I wasn't quite ready to make amends. I knew I'd been in the wrong, but she'd started it. Or her subconscious had started it by bringing up the Lionheart Incident.

I wished I wasn't still so angry about the whole thing with the pony.

The following summer, we'd all had a great time on her next birthday. We had gone horseback riding around Dragonfly Lake—with full-sized, regular horses for all of us girls. That was a happy memory. So why did I fixate on the previous year? I guessed I would never get over the humiliation of being singled out as the chubby girl who was too big for a pony. I would always be that girl, no matter what happened.

Thanks to skipping breakfast, my stomach was rumbling by the time I reached Baker Street.

I stopped in at Donut Joe's, where Rhonda gave me my usual coffee, as well as—I'll admit it—three donuts.

A bit of overindulgence wasn't going to kill me. Not that day. My health was pretty good in general, according to my doctor. I was just one of those girls who carried "a little extra fuel" for emergencies. I was stable and kept it in balance. Knockoff Pop-Tarts and triple-donut breakfasts aside, I did make healthy choices more often than not.

Nisha often praised me for my body positivity, but I described my feelings more as *body neutrality*. My body was how I got around. It was the only one I'd ever have, and it was healthy and worked well. I had my mother's body, and I loved it on her, so why not on me? I wasn't going to sob into a bucket of fried chicken over being too round in some spots, but, on the other hand, I wasn't posting bikini pictures on social media to make a statement, either. I was neutral, which was a perfectly reasonable place to be.

However, as I consumed the first donut in the darkness of a still-closed Bookworm Books, my feelings about my body dipped below neutral. Consuming donut number two did not improve things. By the time I got to donut number three, which my stomach did not want, I was basically committing a hate crime against my body.

On top of that, some needy customer kept calling the store. The phone kept ringing, but I let it go to voicemail. We weren't open yet, and I had my own stuff to deal with. I was in the middle of a hate crime.

After I'd finished all three donuts and licked the crumbs out of the box, I brushed my teeth with the travel toothbrush I kept in my purse. Then I tried not to think about the chewed-up donuts mixing around with digestive juices in my stomach.

I was opening the store and putting the sandwich board on the sidewalk when I saw a petite girl with short brown hair walking toward me. It was Josie, the angry girl from Dalton's past. The one who had taken our picture then sprayed me with my own garden hose on my own lawn.

She saw me spot her, and she slowed down.

I stood my ground.

She turned, pretended to look at something interesting in a store window, then walked the other way.

When I got back into the store, the vintage yellow phone was ringing.

"Good morning, Bookworm Books."

"Is it?" The caller was Dalton Deangelo. "Is it a good morning? It can't be as good as mine. I woke up in a beautiful five-star hotel room, on the most luxurious sheets. I'm about to order room service. Care to join me?"

"Gotta work today," I said. "Plus I already ate three donuts."

He laughed, probably thinking I was joking.

"You're the best," he said. "Hey, so when you went to the ladies' room last night, did you call your best friend to swoop in and rescue you from my evil clutches?"

"Yes," I said. "I got scared."

"Scared of what? I'm not the big, bad wolf. Not unless you want me to be." His voice got thick and low. "Peaches Monroe, do you want me to huff and puff and blow your house down?"

I giggled girlishly and kicked up one foot behind me, Brittany-style. In my defense, I was pretty high on donuts.

There was a long pause, then I heard his muffled voice as he talked to someone else on his side.

"We're going to be filming late tonight, doing some night scenes," he said when he came back. "That's why I called. My schedule got busy. I won't be able to see you until Saturday at the soonest."

"That's too bad. My mom wanted you to come for dinner on Friday. She's making ham."

He groaned. "You're killing me. I love ham."

"Well, duh. Who doesn't love ham?"

"I'd love to see your family again. Say hi to Elliot for me, will you?"

"I will."

"So, I'll see you Saturday?"

"Hang on. Let me check." I did the mental math. Today was Wednesday, which put Saturday three days away. Three days' notice was actually an appropriate amount of time for a gentleman to wait for a date, according to Dottie Simpkins and *The Secret Rules of Love*.

"I can squeeze you in," I said.

With zero hesitation, he said, "I bet you could."

"You'd love that."

"You can squeeze me any way you want," Dalton said. "How about we exchange phone numbers like a couple of normal people, so I don't have to call your store every fifteen minutes, waiting for you to open?"

"That was you? I thought it was a needy customer."

"I *am* a needy customer," he said. I couldn't see him, but I pictured an eyebrow waggle to go with his line.

"If I give you my number, you'd better not give it to your butler."

"You don't like Bernard? His feelings are going to be so hurt by that. He thinks you two are becoming friends."

"Bernard's great. I just don't want him phoning me to arrange... my *fetching* for you. I'm not takeout."

"You could give me Nisha's number. Then I could have my person phone your person. Your roommate seems to have strong opinions about what's good for you."

"Yup," I said hollowly, then I gave Dalton the number for my cell phone. He gave me his as well.

"I promise not to post this in your fan group," I said.

"It's the fifth number I've had this year," he said. "I know you won't post it anywhere, but it always gets out eventually." In the background, there was a hammering sound.

"Are you really in bed in a five-star hotel room?"

"No," he said with a chuckle. "I've been up since four o'clock. It was just wishful thinking. A bit of a fantasy."

"What else was happening in this fantasy?"

"You were here with me," he said.

"Oh, was I?"

"Yes," he said, then he went on to detail what things we might have been doing on the imaginary luxurious sheets in the spacious hotel room.

I fanned my face with my hand. He sure could paint a vivid scene.

The bells on the front door jingled.

A white-curled lady with a coral necklace and matching glasses came in. She browsed the romance novel section of the bookstore. Meanwhile, on the phone, Dalton breathlessly described scenes much hotter than anything in those books.

After a few minutes, the lady approached the counter with her romance novels. I was still on the phone, listening to every breathy word. She coughed politely to get my attention.

"Thank you, sir," I said, cutting off Dalton's story with brisk professionalism. "We'll have that particular item ready for you on Saturday. What time will you be by to, um, fetch it?"

"You must have customers in the store."

"I do."

"Tell me how hot I made you just now."

I replied, "The temperature in the bookstore today is slightly higher than average."

The white-curled lady at the counter raised an eyebrow.

"Glad I could warm you up," Dalton said. "I'll swing by your house Saturday morning. Is ten o'clock too early?"

"Not at all," I said. "I look forward to it."

"Wear hiking boots," he said, then he ended the call.

Chapter 20

Thursday, May 12th

To avoid another donut disaster, I decided to have breakfast at home Thursday morning.

To keep peace in the house, I made a huge omelet to share with Nisha.

My roommate and best friend took three small bites then said, "I'm not very hungry this morning for some reason."

"Nisha, I told you I was sorry for storming off and leaving you at the dog park on Tuesday night."

She stroked her silky black hair and narrowed her brown eyes at me. "Did you? I don't recall that conversation."

"I can't, either, but that doesn't mean it didn't happen."

She scowled, but in a playful way.

"Eat your omelet," I said. "I put every kind of cheese in there, including cheese from a goat. Just how you like it."

She picked at the omelet a little more.

"Dalton and I have a date on Saturday," I said. "He's picking me up here at ten o'clock. He told me to wear hiking boots."

"You can borrow mine," she said.

"No way. Then I'll have to go hiking. I was thinking about wearing strappy sandals and getting him to change his plans. I think spending the day at the Pier would be much better. That's a good date place, right?"

"It's so busy there. People would recognize him, for sure, and hound him for pictures. I'm sure he wants to go out into the woods for a reason."

"Oh." I looked down at my omelet, which had turned out picture-perfect. "I hadn't thought about that."

"It's good to think about other people's feelings sometimes," Nisha said. "Other people have things going on, too."

"I know," I said defensively.

We ate our omelets in silence.

As we were tidying up the dishes, I asked, "What's happening at work? Did Noah say anything about being single and available?"

She frowned at the dishwasher. I could tell she didn't want to talk to me about her boss, but I could also tell she wanted to talk to someone about it.

"He has dropped a few hints," Nisha said.

"Has he been flirting with you again?" Noah always flirted with Nisha when he was in between blondes with nearly flat chests.

She smiled then quickly hid it from me. "Noah and I have a nice friendship, and that's how it's going to stay," she said. "I'd be open to more, of course, but the timing needs to be right. I wouldn't want to be a rebound."

"That man only does rebounds," I said.

She gave me a dirty look. "You don't know him."

"I've met him, and I know what you tell me about him."

She raised her nose in the air. "I exaggerate sometimes." She turned to leave the kitchen. "Have a good day at work. Sell lots of books. Don't let anyone read the last pages."

"That reminds me. I need to put up a sign threatening double-punches to the butt area for any customers who read the last page first. Those people are the worst."

She left the kitchen.

I finished cleaning up, turned on the dishwasher, and stepped outside.

I walked around the side of the house and retrieved the paperback I'd tossed out of my bedroom window during my battle with Nisha on Sunday. Luckily for me and my paperback, it hadn't rained in the last four days.

When I came around the front, Mr. Galloway greeted me as usual.

"Good morning," I said. "Retirement looks great. It must be nice to start your day puttering in the flowerbeds."

"This isn't how I started my day," he said. "I had a grim surprise this morning."

I stopped and tucked my paperback into my purse. This neighborly exchange was going to take a minute.

"I'm sorry to hear that," I said. "Is there anything I can help you with?"

"How are you at extermination?" He pushed his wire-rimmed glasses up his thin, sunburned nose. "I believe a rat has moved into my house. It's been going on for about a week now. I was about to prepare my oatmeal this morning when I found rat excrement on my kitchen counter."

"Are you sure it wasn't chocolate sprinkles? Did you taste them?"

Mr. Galloway stared at me, open-mouthed. He was a nice man, but he did not always get my sense of humor.

"It's probably for the best that you didn't taste them," I said. "How did it get in? You've got that fancy sensor on your cat flap."

"I believe Mr. Whiskers brought the rat inside himself, through the cat door."

"Then it's Mr. Whiskers' problem to exterminate the rat, isn't it? Isn't that the whole point of having a cat? I mean, aside from the amazing conversations."

Mr. Galloway gave me another blank stare.

I said, "If you want, I can pick up a mousetrap at the hardware store while I'm out today."

"That's very kind of you to offer, Peaches, but judging by the size of the, er, chocolate sprinkles, I'd wager he's a big fella. He'd wear one of those little mouse traps as a hat."

"I'm sure Mr. Whiskers will take care of it eventually."

Mr. Galloway leaned his long, beanpole body against the pergola. "I believe they are friends. I came out last night to find Mr. Whiskers watching as the rat dined on his kitty food."

"That sounds adorable. I think we have a children's storybook about a cat and rat who become friends. Did you take a picture?"

"Why would I take a picture? I'm not going to post his mug shot on a Wanted poster." He shook his head and went on. "I won't be able to sleep tonight, wondering what the two of them are up to. Cats and rats should not be friends. The universe has an order. Now, you know I'm not the religious type, but there is a design, and it's beautiful and true. Sometimes the sign comes to you as a number, or sometimes it's a color."

Mr. Galloway wasn't usually so new-age-y. I wondered if Nisha had been loaning him some of her books.

He continued, "The stars are not just in the sky, but in everything, and they do align. Some things do not align."

"What about two people with very different backgrounds?" Such as myself, the bookstore manager, and a famous Hollywood actor.

"You mean like a cat and a rat?" He narrowed his eyes, like he suspected me of making fun of him.

"Never mind. I was just making conversation."

"Watch for a sign," he said. "And don't let anyone eat from your food dish."

"Good advice."

He waved his gloved hand to dismiss me. "Off to work, young lady." He returned to crouching over his perennials.

When I got to the bookstore, I located the children's book I'd mentioned to Mr. Galloway.

The title was *Cat and Rat, Best Friends Forever*.

I settled into a chair and read the book. I noticed some similarities to my own life.

The cat in the story, a peach-colored female, was built for comfort, not for speed. The rat was devilishly handsome, and a real smooth talker.

When the cat closed her eyes for a kiss, the scoundrel rat snuck all his rat friends into the house. He even gave the cat very strong perfume to wear so she wouldn't be able to sniff the rats, and then a beautiful collar, covered in bells.

The stupid cat was so lonely and desperate for love, she didn't suspect a thing.

I couldn't read past the first act. When I returned the book to the shelf, I was near tears. Children's picture books frequently had this effect on me. There was something about raw emotions stated plainly that broke through all my defenses. I suspected it was the same for most people.

We recognize the truth when we see it.

Chapter 21

My mother was disappointed to hear that Dalton wouldn't be joining us for dinner, but she assured me it would still be a nice evening.

I walked into the house and immediately noticed something was different. My mother had been decorating again. The living room had become even more pastel, tightly upholstered, and resistant to napping. My mother was a social woman who loved entertaining her friends in a magazine-perfect formal front room.

A few words about my mother's decorating:

The woman karate-chopped her throw pillows. She bought new wooden things and put an antique paint-chipped finish on them, while simultaneously buying paint-chipped things and refinishing them to a glossy newness. She knew the names of interior decorators who appeared in magazines, and referred to them by first name.

The living room looked great, but it was missing something. My father's beloved recliner. It had lasted through many redecorations, albeit periodically covered in doilies and slipcovers that restricted its natural movement.

I asked, "Where's Dad's chair?"

"In the attic," she said. "I tried to have it hauled to the dump, but he got home from work early and found it on the curb. If only the garbage man had been twenty minutes faster." She shook her head sadly. "He hauled it up to the attic."

"What's he going to do with it up there?"

My mother turned and looked at the bare spot over the fireplace. The television was gone.

"No way," I said. "Dad stole the big TV and hauled it up to the attic?"

"That's not all," she said, frowning and puckering her lips. "He took a mini fridge up there."

"What's the problem? You hated the mini fridge, and you always said that TV was too big. Sounds like you won. You got rid of all the stuff you don't like."

"Along with your father," she said. "Whom I actually *do* like."

"Then I guess you'll be spending more time in the attic. The view's great up there."

My mother leaned in and whispered, "There's no bathroom up there."

"And…? You guys don't have any issues with stairs. You can use the washroom on the main floor."

"I don't mind coming downstairs for that, but I believe your father has been urinating in a bucket up there and throwing it out the window." She shook her head angrily. "Like we're in medieval Europe!"

"Mom! He wouldn't."

She took me over to the window and pointed to the hedge along the house. She pointed to a spot that seemed slightly less lush than the rest of the hedge.

"Look. It's wilting," she said. "That's where he empties the bucket. I'm worried Elliot is going to pick up on the behavior and start doing the same."

"Elliot might be doing it already. It wouldn't take much to influence him. What is it with boys? That kid used to love running around the yard with no pants on, widdling on everything."

She rolled her eyes. "The apple doesn't fall far from the tree."

"Speaking of which, where is the little apple?"

"He's playing at a friend's. He'll come over before bed time and see everyone for a while, but not for too long. I don't want it to be too intense for him."

"Why would that be too intense for Elliot? He loves hanging out with me."

My mother chewed her lower lip. "Since you weren't bringing your new boyfriend, I invited the Stromquists for dinner."

My palms started to sweat. Adrian's parents.

"But not Adrian," I said.

She gave me a confused look. "Why wouldn't I invite Adrian?"

"It would have been nice if you'd warned me," I said. "I could have found an excuse to not be here."

"Don't be silly," she said. "We're all family. And besides, it happened at the last minute. I was at the store today, picking up pineapple for the ham glaze, when I bumped into Astrid." Astrid was Adrian's mother.

I went to the fridge and started rooting around for booze. I poured a vodka and soda, mostly vodka. My mother went to the sink and started washing something. I chugged the drink quickly while Mom's back was turned so I could refill it with another.

She asked, "How are things with the actor?"

"Fine," I said. "He's taking me hiking tomorrow morning."

"Hiking? You don't have to lie to me. If you're meeting him at a hotel for sex, just tell me."

I shot a dirty look at her back. "We're hiking," I said. "Nisha loaned me her boots."

My mother turned around, took the glass from my hand, and sniffed it. "Then I suggest you take it easy on the vodka. It's not cute to vomit in front of a man." She dumped the contents into the empty sink.

"Mom!"

She looked me over then said, "Don't tell people, but when I was your age, I had an affair with someone quite famous."

"What? You were with someone before Dad?"

She nodded for me to pull up a bar stool and get comfortable.

"It was when I was working in art restoration, after college. We had a number of wealthy clients, as you've heard."

"I know," I said. I'd heard about her early career days plenty.

"One day a very famous man came in. I can't say who, but he was desperate. His wife had taken a razor blade to several of his paintings. I wondered what the man had done to deserve such wrath, and then I found out for myself." She looked down, smiling. "Don't tell anyone, but that man seduced me in about twenty minutes flat."

"Stop," I said. "He did not."

"He did," she said. "He took me right there on the workshop table, on top of all the restoration supplies."

I covered my ears with my hands and closed my eyes. But then curiosity took over, and I dropped my hands.

My mother continued calmly. "The affair continued for three weeks. That was the amount of time it took for me to complete the restoration and repair the paintings."

"And then what?"

"He paid the invoice in full, and he also wrote a second check, for me personally." She whispered, "For ten times as much as the restoration bill. He wanted me to stay quiet, because he was back with his wife."

I was on the edge of my bar stool. "What happened next? You didn't cash the check, did you?"

"I did. And I saved the money."

"For what?"

She batted her eyelashes. "Where do you think your father and I got the down payment for this nice house you grew up in?"

"I thought you got a surprise inheritance from some great-aunt who lived across the country."

"That's what we told the neighbors," she said, a sly grin on her face.

I looked down at my now-empty glass. "I'm going to need another drink."

"Pour me one, too."

I did, and my mother and I had a good party going on when the Stromquists arrived.

There were hugs all around. We were family, after all.

Astrid and Erik Stromquist were the grandparents of my "little brother," Elliot Monroe.

Adrian and I were Elliot's birth parents.

Oh, had I not mentioned that Adrian and I hooked up when we were fifteen and foolish? And that it had resulted in the delightful human being my parents were raising as my little brother?

Now you know.

Not many people did. The Stromquists knew, as did some medical personnel and lawyers, but few people outside of the family knew. Even my best friend, Nisha, didn't know. Elliot was only seven, and it wasn't time to reveal the big Monroe family scandal to the world. Not yet.

The six of us gathered around the dining table for a family dinner.

My mom had baked a ham, and it was spectacular.

Chapter 22

Over dinner, Mrs. Astrid Stromquist and my mother talked about orchids.

Mr. Erik Stromquist and my father talked about how amazing it was that more people didn't lose their limbs in radio-control helicopter accidents.

Adrian Stromquist and I didn't talk about anything.

Elliot returned from his friend's house, and the Stromquists spent some time with him. Elliot had grown up calling the family friends Auntie Astrid and Uncle Erik. He didn't find anything unusual about the couple taking so much interest in his life. He was only seven. He only got suspicious about unfamiliar foods that might be hiding vegetables.

After dinner, my mother and Astrid went off together to put Elliot to bed and read him a book.

My father and Erik retreated up to the attic so my father could show off his new setup.

I was washing the dinner dishes in the kitchen when Adrian came in. He said, "What's your beef with me?"

"No beef." I turned on the tap and started filling the sink with hot water to clean the serving bowls.

"You were quiet at dinner."

"I can be quiet sometimes."

"Must be a new thing," he said.

"Must be."

He grabbed a dish towel from the stove. "I'll dry," he said.

"Knock yourself out."

After a moment, he said, "Elliot is a happy kid. I'm glad things worked out."

"It was all pretty easy for you, Adrian. He didn't come shooting out of your babyhole while you were trying to take a bath."

Adrian said nothing. He picked up a bowl and dried it.

I asked, "How's Cujo?"

"He asked me to give you one of these." Adrian used his hand to nip at my bottom.

I had a bowl full of water in my hands. Without thinking, I tossed the water at Adrian. He ducked, and the water soared over his shoulder and splashed on the floor.

Adrian laughed. "Your face," he said. "Priceless."

"What was that all about? You think you can grab my butt whenever you feel like it?"

"It was a gummy bite. From Cujo. He asked me to give it to you. You can't get mad about the last wishes of a dying dog."

"He's dying?"

"Eventually." Adrian gave me one of his smug, know-it-all grins. "He's pretty old."

"You are the worst," I said. "Grab some of the tea towels from this bottom drawer and clean up that water you made me spill." I tapped the drawer with my toe. "Be a civilized adult and take care of the mess you made."

Adrian got the towels, cleaned up the water, then joined me again by the sink.

He said, "Hey, remember when we used to mess around with portraits for the yearbook? Remember how you changed my hair to black and gave me a matching goatee? We called him Evil Adrian."

"I completely forgot about that. You have a good memory."

"Sure do. And I remember how you used to love bubble gum. Either strawberry or watermelon. I still think of you any time I smell either flavor." He picked up the serving plate and dried it. "Those were simpler times. Do you ever wish you could go back and do things differently?"

"Like not make certain decisions? I try not to think about it too much. Elliot's a great kid."

"I mean besides that, obviously."

"My life is great now. I have zero regrets."

"Lucky you," he said, sounding like his old moody, brooding teen self.

"We're too young to have regrets, Adrian. We're too young to have much of anything."

"That's not how I see things."

I stopped washing bowls and turned to him.

Adrian's gaze moved from my eyes to my lips.

I turned away quickly. "The past is the past," I said. "I'm all about looking forward."

"What were you doing up at Dragonfly Lake on Monday night?"

"I told you. I sleep better if I go for a jog in the woods."

"Do you want to go up there with me tonight? I'll be taking Cujo."

"It's an annual event."

"I see." He moved on to the next dish. "Any big plans this weekend?"

"I'm going hiking tomorrow."

Adrian laughed. "No, seriously. What are you up to?"

"I have a date with a famous movie star."

"Peaches, I'm just trying to make conversation. Why do you have to be so difficult?"

The ceiling squeaked. We both looked up.

Adrian asked, "What are they doing up there?"

"I hope my father's not showing your dad his bucket."

"His bucket?"

"Long story," I said. "How are you enjoying living with your folks again after being on your own?"

"The house is lacking," he said. "You should have seen the house I had at the peak of my business. Four thousand square feet. There was a clover-shaped pool in the back yard, as blue as a tropical sky."

"Sounds amazing."

"It was, and yet I still wasn't satisfied. It's lonely in four thousand square feet by yourself."

"Poor Adrian," I said. "You always were moody. You need more sunshine."

"I need someone like you to keep me on my toes." He gave me a sidelong, flirtatious look.

I pretended not to notice he was flirting with me.

Adrian Stromquist had been cute in high school, but now that he'd filled out, he was breaking my brain.

He pulled out the sprayer wand from the edge of the sink and aimed it at my midsection. "Be nice and cheer me up, or you get the hose."

"You wouldn't dare."

He blasted me with lukewarm water—one short burst that rendered my pale-blue T-shirt translucent across my chest.

"You're a monster," I said.

"And you're the winner of our first annual wet T-shirt contest."

I crossed my arms over my wet chest. "Stop eye-groping my peaches."

"That shirt is really see-through when it's wet."

"If you keep looking, I'm sending you an invoice for the peep show."

"You know I'm broke, right?"

"I'm sure you've got some assets hidden somewhere."

He stared at me intensely. "I invite you to search me."

"Then what? If I find any assets I like, should I seize them?"

"Seize them as hard as you'd like."

I turned away.

The ceiling squeaked again.

Adrian said, "I should join the other men in the attic and find out what the bucket is for."

"You don't want to do that."

He nodded at the sink. "The dishes are done. There's not much left for us to do on our own."

"We could play a game."

He blinked his pale eyelashes suggestively. "I thought that was what we were doing."

"This is my life," I said. "It's not a game."

"It's my life, too."

We were facing each other. He had a tea towel in his hand. Without looking down, he gently patted the front of my shirt.

Still holding my gaze, he said, "You're damp."

"Thanks for cleaning up the mess you made."

He kept patting my front with the towel. "Is this okay?"

I nodded. My whole body was getting warmer by the second.

"I got a little on your face," he said softly. He brought the towel up and gently caressed my jaw, first on one side, then the other.

I felt woozy, so I reached out to catch my balance. My hands landed on either side of his waist.

He stepped closer and wiped my neck with the tea towel.

"You're shaking," he said. "Was the water cold?"

I shook my head.

He leaned forward slowly.

I tilted my chin up.

His lips were so close, I could feel his breath.

Then our fathers came charging down the steps from the attic, as loud as buffalo.

Adrian pulled away and turned to the sink. He grabbed the clean, dry dishes and threw them back into the sudsy water.

I ran off to the main floor washroom, where I used my mother's hair dryer on my wet T-shirt.

Adrian hadn't been joking about how see-through it was when wet.

I sat on the edge of the tub and waited for my breathing to calm down.

We had almost kissed.

I had almost let Adrian Stromquist kiss me, right in my parents' kitchen. What was I thinking?

Chapter 23

Nisha asked, "Did you want him to kiss you?"

We were sitting on her bed, discussing my surprising evening with the Stromquists.

Before I could answer, honestly or otherwise, I sneezed from the incense she had burning on her bedside table.

"You did," she said, bouncing up and down as she answered her own question.

"Maybe in that moment," I said. "But not in general. Not Adrian." I wrinkled my nose.

"You two aren't finished with each other in this life," she said. "Your souls are entwined."

"Perhaps," I said. We were entwined, at least genetically. Adrian and I did have offspring together. Nisha didn't know about that. She certainly did have keen insight to be able to recognize it, though. My best friend could be wise about things sometimes, albeit in a nutbar way. I was lucky to have her on Team Peaches.

Nisha closed her eyes. "I can picture it now. Did you say he was patting your chest with a tea towel?"

"Yes. And my face."

Nisha opened her eyes. "That's a very sensual experience for two people to share. I completely understand why he chose that moment to make his move. It was the right thing to do. He can't tell you he's a wee bit in love with you, so he was trying to show you."

"If he wasn't so tall, we would have kissed for sure. It was this close." I held up my fingers to show her how close his lips had been to mine.

She sighed. "I don't know how you're going to choose. I was Team Dalton at first, but I'm leaning toward Team Adrian now. You guys have history."

"What do you mean, Team Dalton or Team Adrian? We've talked about this. You're Team Peaches."

She swished her lips from side to side. "Both guys have their pluses and minuses."

"Do you still think I'm a sex and love addict? Because I think my behavior tonight proves I'm not. After the almost-kiss, I didn't even allow myself to be in the same room alone with Adrian. I stuck to my mother's side like glue."

She raised one impeccable dark eyebrow. "If you didn't fear you had an addiction, you wouldn't be so defensive, and you wouldn't care what I thought."

Her incense smoke was coming right into my face. I fanned it away then took a drink from my bottled water. My mother's ham was amazing, as usual, but it had been salty.

"If I am addicted to bad boys, I got it naturally from my mother," I said.

Nisha wrinkled her nose. "Your dad is not exactly what I'd call dangerous. Not when he's on his own, without those flying chainsaws he's obsessed with."

"Before my mom met him, she had an affair with some famous guy. She told me tonight."

Nisha leaned forward, eyes bright. "Who?"

"I couldn't get it out of her, but I think it was an actor. She did an art restoration for him, and they had a torrid affair."

"Good for your mom." She gave me a wary look. "How long before she met your dad?"

"A couple of years," I said. "Now I know why she gets that funny look on her face whenever she talks about her first year doing art restoration. She's thinking about *him*."

"That will be you in the future. When you're married to a regular guy and you think back to the summer you dated Sir Drake Cheshire. You can tell your kids, and they can be scandalized that their mother was once a creature of sensual desire."

"That's me, all right. Any guy can seduce me with a splash of water and a tea towel."

"Adrian isn't just any guy," Nisha said. "You've always loved him."

"I've always loved Pop-Tarts. That doesn't mean I'm going to end up with them."

"Of course not," Nisha said. "We don't have money for brand-name Pop-Tarts. From now until the end of time, it's all generic-brand Toaster Strudels." She reached over to her side table and put a brass cone over top of the burning incense, snuffing its fragrant smoke. "We both need to get some sleep. You've got hiking in the morning. How are the boots? Did you try them on?"

I frowned. "They fit perfectly. I have no excuse not to go hiking."

"Bring an extra pair of socks." She smirked. "And underwear." She waggled her eyebrows.

"Sure," I said. "But only in case I see a bear, or cannibal Forest Folk, and soil myself."

"Keep telling yourself that," she said with a slow, deliberate blink.

I got up to leave.

"Hang on," she said. "Did you sign that paperwork?"

I gave her a blank stare.

"It's on the kitchen table," she said. "The model release forms. Noah wants to run the big ad campaign focusing on diversity. He wants to use those pictures we took of you in the Penntastic line for curvy yoga practitioners."

"But I don't even do yoga," I said. "He should reshoot them with an actual yoga instructor."

Nisha replied, "But none of our instructors are, *you know*."

"Fine," I said with a weary sigh. "I'll be the token fat girl."

"There's nothing wrong with that," Nisha said. "I'm always the token brown girl in our promotional materials. It's better to be included than excluded."

I rubbed my chin. "You'd think it would be easier for a yoga studio to attract more instructors who are, you know, actually Indian."

"You'd think," Nisha said then shrugged. "Noah has to choose from the people who apply."

"I'll sign the model release, but not for him. I don't like that guy. He's always taking advantage of you, and he doesn't pay you enough. But I'll sign it for you, because I'm Team Nisha."

"Thanks," she said sleepily, fluffing her pillow.

I switched off her light and left her to sleep.

I found the papers in the kitchen and signed them. I was not a model, but about a month earlier, I'd stopped into the yoga studio when they were photographing samples of the clothing they carried. They didn't have anyone handy to try on the larger sizes, so I'd stepped in to represent the curvy girls. I didn't expect they'd ever use the photos for anything.

As I signed the model release, though, I felt something.

Pride.

My first stirrings of body positivity pride.

Chapter 24

Saturday, May 14th

Dalton Deangelo arrived at my house at exactly ten o'clock.

He looked over my hiking outfit—cargo pants, a pink T-shirt, and a plaid overshirt—and said, "That'll do."

He was dressed up like a professional hiker, in camouflage clothes that had all sorts of technical-looking zippers and pockets.

When we got to the car, Dalton opened the front passenger-side door for me.

"Where's Bernard?"

"I gave him the day off. He picked up a local listing for tennis lessons."

"Careful about giving your trusty butler time off," I said. "He might get comfortable here. Then you'll find yourself without a butler when you go back to LA."

"We'll see about that."

He got into the driver's side, and we drove out of the city.

I didn't ask where we were going. I imagined it was one of the many local hiking trails that fitness enthusiasts like Nisha raved about.

"How was filming?" I asked.

"Grueling," he said. "How was the rest of your week at the bookstore?"

"Not bad," I said. "I saw your friend, Josie. She was skulking around outside the bookstore."

"Did she come in and harass you?"

"Nope. Which is too bad, because I had the pepper spray ready."

He said nothing as he stared straight ahead at the road.

After a few minutes, he said, "I have to tell you something." He sounded serious.

"What?" A dozen horrible thoughts raced through my head, including but not limited to the following:

He was married.

He was dying of an incurable illness.

He was leaving town tonight.

He never wanted to see me again.

"My father is a famous actor," he said. "He's known for action films."

"Oh," I said. "I thought you were going to tell me something terrible."

He glanced over at me. "Weren't you supposed to be my biggest fan?"

"Why do I get the feeling I'm failing a test?"

"Think about it," he said.

I did. After a moment, it came to me in a flash. "But you don't come from an acting family," I said. "Your mom worked at the telephone company, and your dad was a long-haul trucker." His parents had passed away a few years earlier, one after the other. He didn't go into details about it in interviews, but I imagined it must have been hard to lose one's parents so young.

"I'm sorry about your parents," I said.

"Thanks," he said, then, "Now you get it."

I got it? I wasn't sure I did. I pulled one of Nisha's granola bars from my purse.

He asked, "You get it, right?"

"Clear as mud," I said, unpeeling the granola bar.

He leaned over and opened his mouth like a baby bird. I offered him a bite of my granola bar, and he took half.

Then he shot me a guilty look.

"I won't tell your trainer," I said. "What's going on with your father? Was he secretly an actor? Did you find out after he died? I hear a lot of family secrets come out that way. Either that way, or when someone sends their DNA to one of those ancestry companies."

"No. Richard Deangelo was never an actor."

"Okay. Was he secretly... not your dad?"

"Bingo," he said. "Richard Deangelo was not my biological father. That honor belongs to Jocko Ranger. You may have heard of him."

"No way! Jocko Ranger? He's one of my mom's favorite actors. At least until... all the recent stuff."

"He was everyone's mom's favorite actor until the recent stuff," Dalton said.

"No kidding." I stared at the handsome young actor's profile, trying to match his features to the older and much more famous actor. "I see it now. The family resemblance." I took a nibble from the granola bar. "Do people know?"

"I didn't even know until a few years ago. As for the general public, they're going to know soon enough."

"Does this rift between you and your friend have anything to do with Jocko Ranger's big scandal?"

Dalton stared straight ahead. "You mean the scandal where Jocko's daughter sold the tabloids a private phone message of Jocko having a nervous breakdown?"

"I listened to that recording. He didn't sound very nervous. He sounded like a bigot, on top of a few things." I shook my head. "I'm sorry your dad's like that."

"He's not like that," Dalton said defensively. "The message got edited to sound worse than it was."

"But he still said those words."

"Jocko Ranger is not a saint, but he's not as bad as that message."

I didn't say anything for a minute. Then I said, "I'm not in your shoes, Dalton. Or Jocko Ranger's. It must be tough to be in the spotlight. You can't slip up at all or it's everywhere. I wouldn't get away with half the stuff I do if anyone cared who I was."

Dalton nodded slowly and stared at the road ahead.

We drove for a minute in silence, then I gasped and smacked my forehead. "The angry girl that you sprayed with a garden hose on my lawn was Josie *Ranger*. Jocko Ranger's daughter. The one who did some singing on that reality TV show, in between stints in rehab."

"That's the one," Dalton said.

"She's your sister," I said.

"She's my half sister."

"Wow. It's quite the family tree you've got."

"It's complicated."

"Why was Josie Ranger trying to take your picture?"

"Josie doesn't always have the best ideas. Remember, she's the one who sold the phone recording of our father for drug money."

"Yikes."

"But then she got cleaned up, supposedly, and she wanted to make amends. She wanted all of us, including me, to do a big-happy-family piece in a major magazine. She wanted us to come out about our relationship. She thinks it will rehabilitate her father's reputation and get him working again."

"But he is working. He's got a new movie coming out."

"That was already in the works before the phone message scandal hit. Let's just say his agent's phone isn't ringing off the hook." He glanced over. "Just between us, the new movie is going to be a stinker."

"So why not help the guy out?"

"You think I should pose for publicity photos with my father, the action movie star who's seen better days, and my half-sister, the desperate B-lister who sells out her family for drug money?"

"When you put it that way, it doesn't sound very appealing." I glanced out at the passing terrain. We were on the outskirts of the city, where the land became wild and green. "Then again, don't they say all publicity is good publicity?"

"They don't say that anymore," he said. "That was a saying back before internet mobs demanded for people to be struck down from popular culture for crossing boundaries."

"Things are different now," I said. "But people still love a good redemption story. And they love to see family pulling together. The world is changing, but that stuff is forever."

"You're very wise for the ripe old age of twenty-two, Peaches Monroe."

"I read a lot of books. You know the saying. A reader gets to live countless lives."

"You could say that about actors."

"You could." I stared out at a farm field we were passing by. "So why not do the publicity with your father? You probably would help him out. Your reputation is pretty clean, considering what a bad boy you are."

He shot me a playful look. "My publicist said no. It's not the right time. My people feel that, at the current moment, my father would only drag me down with him."

"And your half-sister didn't take that well?"

"Not well at all. Ever since then, she's been trying to humiliate me."

"That's not fair of her. You can't do things that are bad for your career, not even if you do like your dad. Do you like your dad? What's Jocko Ranger like in real life?"

Dalton pursed his lips. "That's a topic for another day. I want today to be about us. It doesn't matter how different we are. Let's just be two souls together. Two souls who are made of stardust, and found their way back to each other, the way they were destined to."

"Is that a line from your movie?"

He grinned. "I can't say. It's top secret."

"What other secrets are you hiding, Dalton Deangelo? What was going on with those reporters the day you came running into my bookstore and swept me off my feet?"

"Ah. That," he said. "Those reporters were working on a tip Josie gave them. It wasn't true at all, but it still took the idiotic press a couple of days to figure out Josie's word wasn't reliable."

"She's really got it in for you," I said. "When she grabbed my arm on the lawn and tried to warn me about you, that seemed like it was about more than a failed publicity stunt."

"She wanted to hurt me by scaring you off," Dalton said.

"You're not a notorious womanizer, breaking hearts left and right?"

"Not lately," he said.

"She was right to warn me about you."

He glanced over and gave me a hurt look. "The truth is, I've been so busy working that I haven't even dated anyone in almost a year."

"But you're always going to events with gorgeous skinny girls on your arm."

"Friends and co-stars," he said. "The truth is, I've been a little cautious since..." He trailed off.

"Since what? Or should I say, since *whom*?"

He shot me a guilty look. "Since the Jade incident."

He meant the famous pop singer whose poster had been on every guy's wall when I was growing up. She was older now, but her posters still sold like hotcakes.

"No way," I said. "That was real?"

"What did you hear?"

"The story in the press was that you were dating Jade in LA while she was on that singing show, and then her husband flew down there and punched you in the face."

"Sounds about right."

"Really? I thought that was just a publicity stunt, or one of those made-up stories."

"That one's real." He shot me another guilty look before returning his attention to driving.

"I can't believe I slept with a guy who slept with Jade," I said with wonder. "That's amazing."

"You're not jealous?"

"It's Jade," I said. "Given the chance, I'd probably sleep with her, too." I paused and snorted. "But not while she was married. How could you? She has kids. She..."

My mind went blank then rebooted.

"Sugar!" The puzzle pieces fell into place in my head.

Dalton said, "In my defense, Jade told me the marriage was over and that they were separated. I didn't know that only she and her lawyer knew about the separation, and that she hadn't told her husband yet. I'm not perfect, but I'm not *that* bad."

I slipped down on the leather seat as my brain rebooted. I finally got everything back online and said, "Garnet."

"What?"

"The dark-haired kid who works for me part-time at the bookstore. Garnet Langtree. He's Jade's son. That explains why he was so rude to you last Saturday."

"That kid with the dark hair is Jade's son? Wow. Talk about a crazy coincidence."

"I'll say."

"You slept with Garnet's mom," I said.

"I didn't know. I mean, yeah, I knew she had kids, but she told me the marriage was over."

"How did you even meet?"

"We know a few people in common. We met the usual way, at an industry thing. Champagne may have been involved."

"Did you love her?"

He didn't answer for a while, then said, "She's a complicated woman."

"That's how women are." I looked out the window again. "She's my employee's *mom*."

We drove in silence for a few minutes.

Then I said, "Nisha doesn't believe in coincidences. She says our life threads weave around each other in a deliberate way. She would say that you didn't run into my bookstore *despite* Garnet but *because of him*. She would say that fate sent you in there because you need to make amends with Garnet for tearing his family apart."

"Nisha has some interesting ideas." He tapped on the steering wheel. "I'm not going to do that," he said. "How would that even look? What would I do?" He shook his head. "No way. It's better to let sleeping dogs lie. I have been scandal-free for almost a year, and it's going to stay that way."

I didn't say anything.

He leaned over and squeezed my knee. "We're just going to have a nice hike up to the Weston Estate, soak in their secret hot spring, and forget all about Hollywood, and the internet, and all the insanity."

"Did you say *secret hot spring*? On the Weston Estate?"

"I did."

"But that's not real. It's just an urban legend."

He gave me a playful look. "If you want to know what's real and what's not real in this world, you have to see it for yourself." He squeezed my knee again. "And feel it for yourself."

Chapter 25

We reached the turn-off for the Weston Estate.

Dalton turned onto the road, completely ignoring the multiple posted signs forbidding trespassing.

We approached an enormous sign, which Dalton read out loud in a dramatic announcer voice. "*You're not lost. You're trespassing. Turn around now and go back the way you came.*"

"That sign could not be more clear," I said.

Dalton stopped the vehicle and took a picture of the sign.

"You got your souvenir photo," I said. "Now let's turn around, go back into the city, and do something legal. Do you like bowling? That's a dumb question. Everyone loves bowling."

"We're *going* to the hot spring."

"How do you know it's even real?"

"I have my ways." He kept driving on the rutted country road. "I hear the spring has magical restorative powers."

"Oh, yeah? I hear Old Man Weston has quite the shotgun collection and doesn't take kindly to people trespassing on his land."

Dalton slammed on the brakes, put the car in reverse, then took a left turn onto what looked like anything but a road.

I squealed and held on tight to the dashboard. The luxury car bounced and rocked over the rutted terrain.

"Your poor car!" I warbled, my voice broken up by the bouncing.

"I suppose my four-wheel-drive truck might have been a better option."

"You have a truck?"

"For towing my boat."

"Of course you do." I looked over my shoulder at the road through which we'd come. It was a smooth highway compared to the path we were on now.

"Almost there," he said.

"How would you know? This path is completely overgrown. Nobody's driven this way in months."

"Aerial surveillance," he said cryptically.

We bumped along through the bushes. Low-hanging branches whacked the windshield. I worried about the car's suspension, but it kept on going. I imagined how horrified Bernard would be about what his boss was doing to the vehicle.

"Here we are," Dalton said as we lurched to a stop. "This is as far as we can go in the car. Good thing you have your hiking boots." He opened his door. "Let's go!"

I got out of my side. "What the heck," I said. "One day I can scandalize my children with this story."

"There's the spirit."

He got a deluxe backpack from the trunk of the car, pulled it on, and we set out.

"This is nice," he said, pausing to kiss my forehead as we walked along a narrow path through the woods.

"It is nice," I agreed. "I know you just told me all that stuff about Jocko Ranger and your half-sister, and how you slept with Garnet's mom and tore up his family, but being out here in the woods makes that whole conversation in the car feel like something that happened in a different lifetime."

"It did happen in a different lifetime." He gave me a sweet look. "It was B.P. That stands for Before Peaches."

I rolled my eyes.

He took my hand and helped me across a stony section of the trail.

"Well, those are all of my skeletons," he said. "What about yours?"

I shrugged. "What you see is what you get."

He raised his eyebrows. "Is it really? I get all of this?" He looked over my body greedily.

"You have a one-track mind, Dalton Deangelo."

"I blame you," he said. "You and your luscious peaches."

I covered my chest with my forearms. "Stop ogling me. You're so desperate. I'm wearing a sports bra. They're all squished together."

"I know," he said. "They can't wait to be free to bob around in the hot springs."

"Um. *Bob around?* My peaches are real, Dalton. They're not full of helium or whatever it is the girls use in LA."

He grinned and picked up the pace.

Birds chirped all around us. The Weston Estate was huge and beautiful. We weren't hiking for long when I noticed a change in the air. Moisture. I checked the sky for signs of rain clouds, but it was all blue beyond the leaves.

We stepped into a clearing dotted with a few boulders. Up ahead, near a rock outcropping, was a plume of steam.

"Told you so," Dalton said.

"Holy pork chops, the hot springs are real!"

I jogged toward the pool of water. I could have screamed, but we were trespassing, after all.

Dalton raced ahead of me. He shrugged off the backpack, pulled off his boots and hiking pants, then stood near the edge of the water on the rocks in his underwear and T-shirt.

"Be careful," I called out. "Check the temperature. Make sure it isn't boiling hot. You're no good to anyone if you're soup stock."

He pulled off the rest of his clothes and stood naked at the edge of the springs. Butt naked.

"I'll check the temperature," he said, and then he jumped in.

He disappeared beneath the water line.

I was all alone in the woods. The songbirds in the nearby branches sang their tattle-tale songs. Trespassers! Naughty, naked trespassers!

Dalton shot up from the water like a majestic merman, tossing his head back in a spray of water. His skin was rosy.

"You look pink," I said. "Is it boiling hot?"

"Jump in and find out."

I sat near the edge and took off my shoes and socks. I dipped a few toes in cautiously.

Dalton sank down for a mouthful of water then spat it at me in an arc.

I dodged the water. "Don't drink that filth. Isn't warm water basically a party town for bacteria? That hot puddle is a petri dish."

Dalton wiped water from his grinning face. "I wasn't so great at science, but this isn't agar."

"Agar?" I kicked water at his face. "Sounds like you know plenty about science."

"I'm not as dumb as I look."

"Who said you look dumb?"

He fixed me with a serious gaze, his green eyes never looking more enticing than now, surrounded by wild grasses and flowers as steam rose up from the natural hot spring.

"Take off your clothes and get in here with me," he commanded.

"Pass."

Something dark shifted at the edge of my vision. I turned, expecting to see Old Man Weston with a shotgun.

It wasn't him, or any human.

A deer stepped out of the trees. A mother deer with a pair of tiny newborn fawns. They were spotted with their baby colors, and walking tentatively on spindly legs.

The deer gave us a curious look then walked over to the stream running away from the spring's pool. With her big eyes watching me warily, she lowered her head and took a drink. The babies didn't drink. They had their preferred supply of their mother's milk.

And then, just as calmly as she'd arrived, the mother deer gave a flick of her tail and disappeared back into the woods with her adorable offspring teetering behind her.

I let out the breath I'd been holding.

"That was a sign," Dalton said. "From the universe, straight to Peaches Monroe. Now take off your clothes and get in here with me before I climb out of here like an angry sea monster and drag you in."

I pulled my pink T-shirt off over my head.

"Don't watch," I said, but of course that only made him watch me more intently. "Too bad there's no changing room out here. If I owned this estate, I'd put in a cabana."

"Mm hmm."

I could feel the heat of his gaze on me.

"Stop watching," I said.

He didn't. He whistled and hooted, "Take it off!"

I shimmied out of my cargo pants, still facing him rather than offering a side or back view.

"Careful," I said. "You should avert your eyes now or you'll be blinded by the sun reflecting off all my pale flesh."

He waded to the near side of the rocky pool and rested his elbows on the edge, his chin in his hands.

"I could watch you undress all day," he said. "Wear more layers next time."

I was down to my underwear. Should I wear that into the water? Dalton's underwear lay next to the springs with his clothes. When he stepped out, he'd have dry underwear.

I'd brought spare socks and clothes, but they were back in the car, where I'd forgotten them. I decided to keep my underwear on for now. Hiking back to the car with damp underwear was a small price to pay for not being nude in the broad light of day, while trespassing.

"This is the whole show," I said, approaching the steaming spring in my underwear. "There won't be any... bobbing for peaches."

"Whatever you're comfortable with," he said, taking a lighter tone. "I've been naked in front of film crews so many times I've lost track."

"Fully naked? I thought actors wore something over Brazil."

"Brazil?"

I explained the in-joke I had with Nisha as I lowered myself into the water. The water was hot, but not too hot. It was perfect. No wonder the urban legends about the Weston Estate hot springs persisted.

"There are stickers to cover Brazil," Dalton said.

"Do you use them?"

"Of course." He gave me a serious look. "In every interview where reporters ask about sex scenes, actors lie and say they're not sexy at all. And, most of the time, they aren't. But sometimes they are. Having a piece of rigid material glued around Brazil is a good way to keep fantasy separate from reality."

I settled back on a natural rock shelf that made a perfect seat. "Do they really glue it on there?"

"Sort of. It's more like sticky tape." He grimaced. "The adhesive is not hair-friendly."

"It's a good thing you're not very hairy." I pointed to the top of his buff, hairless chest.

"You have no idea how much money this cost," he said. "Laser hair removal." He grinned. "You know how Jocko Ranger is famous for that full chest of curly dark hair? I inherited the chest-hair gene from him."

"My mom loves a hairy chest. My dad's is all red. She calls him her baboon."

"That's cute. You can call me whatever you want."

"Thanks, babe."

He grinned and splashed some water at me. "Why are you all the way over there?"

"I'm taking my time to enjoy this magical setting," I said. "You did bring me out here to enjoy nature, didn't you?"

He stayed where he was. "Enjoy away." He used his hands to make a miniature water cannon. He splashed water outside of the spring.

"This water is so clear," I said. "It's just a hole in the ground. You'd expect it to be muddy."

"This spring has been here thousands of years. Millennia, even. All the mud washed away long ago, before the Westons owned this place. At one time, prehistoric creatures came here to take a dip."

"You did your research."

"I always research my roles."

I raised an eyebrow. "This is a role?"

"The role of a lifetime. How's my audition so far?"

"You might get a callback," I said. "Is that the right word?"

"It is. You've been doing your research, too."

"We have a book at the store about breaking into acting. I may have leafed through it during slow times at the store." When I wasn't having my heart broken by reading *Cat and Rat, Friends Forever*.

Dalton frowned. "I think my side's cooling down. Is it still hot over there?"

"About the same. How could your side be cooling down?"

"Beats me. Do I have permission to come over there, where it's still hot?"

"Oh." I smiled. "Sure. If you think you can keep Brazil under control."

"What's the fun in that?"

He slid over to my side, where he discovered the sitting shelf. "This is the good side," he said.

He draped one arm around my shoulders and nuzzled my ear.

He murmured in my ear, "How are you enjoying our hike?"

"If this is hiking, I might need to get my own pair of boots. I borrowed Nisha's. I never saw myself as a hiker, but, then again, I never saw myself as a trespasser."

"I can take you trespassing as often as you'd like." He began kissing my neck.

I turned to face him and kissed him back.

He pulled me toward him in the warm water, so I was sitting on his lap.

His hands moved over my body slowly.

The water was steaming all around us.

Something buzzed nearby.

I thought it might have been an insect, but it got louder.

We stopped kissing and looked around.

A drone was hovering ten feet away. It was almost as large as its flying predecessors, the flying chainsaw helicopters my father sold parts for. The smaller propellers made the modern drone much less dangerous, but it was still a shock to see it hovering over us.

Chapter 26

The drone kept hovering. We had been discovered.

"Busted," I said to my naked fellow trespasser. "I guess our fun is over. I hope you have a good lawyer to get us out of trespassing charges."

Dalton had his hand up, shielding his face. "Hand me something," he said in a whisper. "Throw me a T-shirt to cover my face."

Indignantly, I said, "What about my face?"

He was already moving, emerging from the hot spring and draping his T-shirt over his head.

He reached down and helped me out.

The drone dipped and buzzed angrily.

"Yeah, yeah," I said to the drone. "We're going. Message received."

That was when speakers on the drone crackled to life with what seemed to be a pre-recorded message: "Attention trespassers. Motion sensors have detected unauthorized activity. A security team is on its way to this site. Please vacate the premises immediately."

Motion sensors? How many cameras were out here? I had just climbed out and was now soaking wet in my underwear, feeling very big and conspicuous.

The recording repeated itself. The phrase "security team is on its way" put some speed in my movements.

Dalton slipped on his underwear and his boots. He still had his shirt over his head, blocking his face from the hovering drone. He hoisted his backpack onto one shoulder, then grabbed our clothes and bundled them in his arms. He pointed to my borrowed boots.

I pointed to my clothes in his arms.

"Forget your clothes," he said. "Just get your boots on so we can run out of here."

"Run?"

"Run," he said.

The gravity of the situation hit me. We were going to run, wet and half naked, fleeing a hovering drone and an incoming security team.

I let out a streak of swear words.

By some miracle I got my wet feet into my borrowed boots.

Then the two of us were off and running through the forest trail. In our underwear.

"Faster," he urged.

The water had rendered my sports bra useless. My peaches were flying everywhere, threatening to knock me out. I clamped down on them with folded arms.

As we ran through the bushes, with evil whipping branches whacking me on all my sensitive areas, I continued my panicked refrain of yelling every swear word I knew.

Dalton interrupted. "Just breathe. Swearing doesn't make you run faster."

"Says you." I continued to do what worked for me.

"They're probably bluffing," Dalton said calmly between breaths. "I bet there's no security team coming."

Over the sounds of us crashing through the woods, I could swear I heard another noise. Was it a couple of men talking to each other in what sounded terrifyingly like the SWAT team lingo I'd heard in action movies? Or were my ears playing tricks on me?

I began swearing harder and faster. Contrary to what Dalton believed, it did make me run faster.

"Shortcut," he panted. He grabbed my hand and hauled me sharply to the side, off the very rough trail and onto what wasn't even a trail at all.

Now the tree branches and bushes really started slapping my bare flesh, whipping me. I knew some people were into that sort of thing, but not this gal.

"We're almost there," Dalton said.

I had to stop to catch my breath. I leaned against a tree. "Go on," I panted. "Save yourself. Leave me here. I'll take the rap for both of us."

"Come here. I'll carry you."

He was strong and could carry me, but how far? The horror of him attempting to get me all the way back to the car prompted me to get moving again. The trees kept whipping me. My wet sports bra continued to be ineffective.

Was that a glint of metal up ahead?

It was!

I had never been so happy to see a car as when we emerged from the bushes and found Dalton's car waiting for us.

We yanked the doors open and jumped into the seats, our damp bodies making rude noises on the leather.

Dalton started the car and did a prolonged ten-point turn to get us headed in the right direction.

As we rolled off down the trail again, he turned to me, his eyes wide, and started howling with laughter.

"We made it," I said.

We bounced up and down as the car drove over bumps and ruts on the rough trail.

He kept laughing.

I asked, "What's so funny?"

"Look at yourself," he said. "You're dressed in a green bodysuit."

I looked down, surprised to find I was covered in green leaves and flower petals. Dalton had barely anything stuck to him.

I demanded, "Why are you clean? Did you towel off when I wasn't looking?"

"You were in front of me, clearing the path," he said.

"Very funny," I said with a snort. I was not amused. "Put the big girl in front to clear the path. Real nice."

"Are you mad?"

I crossed my arms. "We could have gotten shot back there. You heard those commandos in the security team."

"There was no security team," he said. "It was an automated system."

"I heard them."

"Your imagination heard them," he said. "Why would anyone waste money on a security team to protect a little hot spring?"

"We shouldn't have been trespassing," I said angrily. "Just because you're a Hollywood hotshot and your dad's Jocko Ranger, that doesn't make you above the law."

"Peaches." He gave me a pouty look. "Don't be mad."

"I'm not mad. Just tired." We drove for a moment in silence, then I said, "I'm not really that out of shape. I go to the gym sometimes, and I walk absolutely everywhere. I just don't do a lot of running. Obviously."

"You kept up just fine." The rough road was tricky, so he had his eyes straight ahead.

"I'm not sure I want to keep up with you," I said.

"There are towels in my backpack. Why don't you get yourself dried off and see if that improves your outlook?"

The backpack was in the back seat, so I started climbing over the divider to get back there.

Dalton didn't pass up an opportunity to gently bite me on my buttocks as they passed by his head.

I was still angry about trespassing and being forced to run, but, weirdly, the playful bite didn't push me over the edge. Some part of me had known he would do that, and it was why I'd wriggled over the divider rather than ask for the car to be stopped so I could go by the door.

All things being equal, I'd rather be with a guy who wanted to bite me on my butt than one who wasn't interested in it.

I reached the back seat, removed the foliage from my front, dried off, and got my pink T-shirt, flannel overshirt, and cargo pants back on.

I was still damp from my underwear, but I felt better with a layer of fabric covering everything.

My driver called back over his shoulder, mimicking Bernard's accent, "Everything okay back there, ma'am?"

"I'm okay."

I crawled back up front. He bit me again. I didn't mind at all.

We had left the Weston Estate and were back on a regular road again.

"Running always works up my appetite," he said. "Is there anywhere good around here to get lunch?"

"There are plenty of places back in the city. As for out here, in the boonies, there's not much. I mean, there's a truck stop that sells mile-high pies, but I don't know if it's your kind of place."

"I could go for a mile-high pie," he said.

We punched the name of the place into the navigation and were there in fifteen minutes.

Dalton got dressed in the vehicle, and we went in.

After we had finished eating our meal, Dalton leaned back with a contented expression on his face and said, "This place gets five stars from me."

"You don't have to say stuff like that," I said. "You don't have to pretend to like blue-collar things around me."

"I'm not pretending," he said.

The gum-chewing waitress came over and refilled our coffee cups. She splashed on both of the saucers and didn't say anything about the mess.

After she'd walked away, Dalton said, "I'm taking my rating down to four stars due to the service."

"Did you go to a lot of places like this with your dad? Not the actor, but the one who was a long-haul trucker?"

"I went on a couple of short runs with him, but my mother didn't like me being away. She didn't like being alone."

I sipped my bitter diner coffee. I'd never tasted a brew more burned than that one. My rating went down to three stars.

"If I'm out of line, just say so, but I need to ask," I said. "How did your mother manage to hook up with Jocko Ranger?"

"Before she worked at the phone company, she worked at a jewelry store. He came in one night when they were closing, and he asked her to keep the store open a little longer so he could find something for his wife's birthday."

"Say no more," I said. "I get the picture."

"Can I tell you anyway? I haven't been able to talk about it much. It helps to talk about it. She told me on her deathbed. That was... difficult."

"Sure," I said, swallowing down the lump in my throat. It was hard to imagine Dalton sitting by his mother's bed that way.

He smiled, his emerald-green eyes twinkling with amusement. "You should have seen her the night she told me. She was so weak at the time, but she came to life with the memory." He looked down at his cup of bitter coffee. "I guess that's the point of memories."

"I'm glad she was able to share that with you."

He chuckled hollowly. "Oh, she shared it, all right. More detail than I would have liked." He glanced up and held my gaze, his gorgeous eyes shining. "They were alone together in the back room, where she was making adjustments to the setting of a necklace, and according to her, he seduced my mother in twenty minutes flat."

I stopped breathing. "Excuse me?"

"From the moment he walked into the jewelry store to the moment he took her on the workbench, it had been exactly twenty minutes. He bragged to her that it was his personal record."

"That sounds awfully familiar," I managed to say. It sounded an awful lot like my mother's encounter with an unnamed celebrity. With a squeaky voice, I asked, "What city was this?"

"New York," he said. "That's where I grew up, before I made the big move west to California. Aren't you my biggest fan? I thought you knew that."

I stared at him, dumbfounded.

"Jocko saw my mother a few times after that," he said. "But not for long. His wife at the time found out, and she went crazy. She burned a bunch of his suits, and she slashed some of his artwork with a razor blade."

A choking sound came out of my throat, but no words.

I would have to check with my mother and confirm the details, but in that moment, there was no doubt in my mind that my mother had been seduced by the same man who'd done the same thing to Dalton's mother.

Facts and assumptions collided in my head. I'd taken my mother's word for it when she'd said the affair had happened before she met my father and had me, but was that the truth? Was there a chance that, like Josie Ranger, I was also Dalton's half-sister?

I leaned forward and asked, "What year was this?"

"It was the year before I was born," he said. "Obviously."

"Stop joking around. I'm serious. What year?"

He picked up his coffee cup and took a sip. "That's a secret," he said playfully. "An actor goes to great lengths to obfuscate his age."

Chapter 27

Sunday, May 15th

My mother stared at me, her expression frozen.

We were sitting in the breakfast nook in the kitchen, having scones and tea. My father had taken Elliot with him to the hardware store and other errands.

My mother finally spoke. "It's a shame it's too early for wine."

"So, is it true? Was Jocko Ranger the man who... gifted you with the down payment for this house?"

"He didn't tell me how to use the money," she said.

"And what year did the affair happen?"

She named a year that was five years before my birthday. It was the year before Dalton had finally admitted to having been born—not that I'd believed him. Hollywood stars tended to lie and make themselves younger than they were, not older, but once the idea we could be related had entered my head, it had been impossible to shake.

"I'm not Jocko Ranger's," I said with a sigh.

My mother rolled her eyes. "Look at yourself in a mirror. Of course you aren't Jocko's."

"It's probably for the best," I said, recovering from my paranoid state quickly. "I like having a non-hairy chest."

"Is that what you were so desperate to talk to me about?" Her blue eyes narrowed at me. "You wanted to come over here and accuse your poor mother of deceiving you about your origins?"

"You did it to Elliot."

She shook her head. "We all agreed that was for the best, at least until he's a little older." She held a hand to her heart. "I'm hurt you would even think that about me."

"So, Jocko Ranger," I said. "And here I thought you saw all his movies because you liked action films."

"I do like action films," she said. "If Jocko Ranger is in them."

"Does Dad know?"

She smiled. "He does. That's why he always gets in shape whenever a new Jocko Ranger movie is coming out. It keeps him on his toes. His doctors always tell him he has the healthy heart and lungs of a much younger man."

"You use jealousy as a tool to keep Dad young and healthy?"

She picked up her scone. "Why not? I wouldn't go to my swim classes if he didn't fawn over Astrid Stromquist so much."

"You guys are so weird. Please don't screw up Elliot too bad."

She rolled her eyes and ate her scone. "You turned out just fine," she said. "I have a perfect daughter."

"Your perfect daughter went trespassing on the Weston Estate yesterday. The hot spring is real. We went for a dip and got chased out of there by security drones."

She gave me a surprised look. "That boyfriend of yours sure knows how to show you a good time." Her expression turned serious. "I do hope you're being careful, Peachy."

"We ran out of there fast, and the security team didn't catch us."

"You know what I mean," she said.

"We're being safe."

"So, you are sleeping with him," she said, looking away.

"There hasn't been a lot of sleeping."

"Oh, Peachy." She made a tsk-tsk. "I suppose I can't blame you. If he's anything like his father..."

We both looked away.

I said, "I miss the good ol' days when I lied to you about my sex life and you didn't tell me about yours."

She replied, "I suppose the cat is out of the bag now." She sipped her tea. "When is Dalton going to come for dinner?" She fanned her cheeks. "I can't believe I'm going to meet Jocko Ranger's secret son. Dalton was already a little boy when I was having you, Peachy. I bet he was an adorable kid."

"You already met him, at the wedding."

"But I didn't know he was Jocko Ranger's son then, did I?"

"Keep that under wraps," I said. "It is a secret."

"I'm telling your father, of course, but he won't tell anyone." She leaned forward eagerly. "When can we see him again?"

"He's pretty busy filming, but we'll see."

"And what about Adrian?"

"What *about* Adrian?"

"Do you still have feelings for him?"

"I'll always feel something for Adrian, because of our connection, but not like that."

She gave me a sly smile. "Astrid told me you two almost kissed in the kitchen."

"He told his mother about that?"

"She came out to get some water and saw you. She said you would have kissed, if you'd had another minute. I understand the fellows came down from the attic and interrupted. Astrid told me you were staring up at her son with love in your eyes."

"Astrid has a wild imagination," I said. "Paired with wishful thinking."

"You two make beautiful babies together."

I got up from the chair. "That's enough. I'm not in love with Adrian."

"No, but you might be after you're finished with Jocko Ranger's son. When he moves on, Adrian will still be here."

"Ugh." I went to the fridge for orange juice.

"There's no rush," my mother said. "Whatever is meant to be will happen, in due time."

"Just because you ended up with a regular guy instead of the famous one doesn't mean I'm going to follow in your footsteps and live a totally ordinary, boring life."

My mother said nothing.

When I looked at her, I could see that I'd hurt her feelings.

I brought the orange juice back to the table and apologized.

She took a moment to compose herself then said, "Whatever happens, your father and I just want you to be happy."

"You mean happily married to Adrian Stromquist."

"That's what your father would like to see happen," she said. "I'm more open minded." She put her chin in her hand and looked up at the ceiling, smiling. "Jocko Ranger's son. Imagine that!"

Chapter 28

Nisha tapped timidly on the frame of my bedroom door.

With my face still in my pillow, I waved in the general direction of my closet. "Help yourself. Borrow whatever you want for your top half." Nisha's top half was about the same size as mine, though her lower half was much smaller.

She came in but didn't go to my closet. She sat on the edge of my bed and asked, "How are you feeling? Was your sleep disrupted at all?"

I sat up, on high alert. "What's going on?"

"So, you can feel it," she said in a breathy, dreamy voice. "You were probably dreaming about it."

"I was dreaming about ham," I said. "But you're acting stranger than usual, so I know something's up. What is it? Just spill it. Don't make me wrestle it out of you."

She took a full breath then said plainly, "There are half-naked photos of you all over the internet."

Every sweat gland in my body pumped its guts out. The world went dark, pulling into a pinhole of light. My mouth watered. The sweet relief of fainting, however, did not come.

"Show me," I said, my voice cold and detached.

She pulled up a page on her phone and handed it to me.

There were a series of photos. It was me, all right. I was wearing the wet sports bra and underwear I'd worn into the hot spring two days earlier, with Dalton. There were photos of us from all angles, from every moment of our hot spring adventure.

Dalton's famous face was covered with his shirt when we were on our way out, but the security cameras had captured plenty before the drone had appeared. Of course they had. If Dalton Deangelo hadn't been recognizable, the photos never would have run.

I scrolled down and read the comments. I shouldn't have.

The article had included my name, so now the people of the internet were making up nicknames for me.

One of the posts had a whole list of awful names for me, as well as a poll. People were voting.

In third place was Porky Peaches.

Second most popular was Peachalicious.

And leading the polls was... Peaches by the Pounds.

I'd been called names before, but this was a whole new level.

Nisha figured out what I was doing and yanked the phone away from me, but it was too late.

A part of me died. Perhaps it was the last shreds of my youthful naivete. Or my faith in humanity. Either way, it died.

I fell back on the bed. If this had been just another comedic moment in my always-hilarious life, I might have made some perfectly witty comment.

Instead, I stared at the ceiling and silently began to weep.

I wept not just about this time and these nicknames, but about every single time people had been cruel to me about my appearance. When I caught my breath, the ragged sobs began.

Chapter 29

Bless her heart, Nisha knew just what to do.

She didn't argue with me about how bad I ought to be feeling, but she did take away my phone and laptop so I couldn't jump further down the black hole.

I cycled through the emotional stages rapidly, with the bargaining stage lasting only twenty minutes.

Nisha did a cleansing ritual, burning some things while chanting, and eventually declared me safe to leave the house.

"Poor Dalton," I said as I was putting on my shoes to leave. "This isn't going to have any effect on my career, but I'm sure his stock is going to go down."

"Come back here," Nisha said, shaking her head and pointing at the kitchen chair. "It sounds like I failed to purge all your negative self-talk." She started rearranging items on the table. "We're going to need a lot more candles."

"You'll have to purge me later," I said. "I need to get to work."

"It's still early," she said. "Are you planning to go to Donut Joe's for your feel-bad ritual of three donuts?"

"Yes."

She crossed her arms. "Peaches."

"Excuse me, ma'am." I waved my finger. "My full name is Peaches by the Pound."

"That sounds like a stripper name."

"So does my regular name."

She held up two fingers. "You can have this many donuts. Two. I'll have something figured out for when you get home, but I can only handle so much bad *ama*."

I promised to be sensible with my donut ordering, then left the house.

When I got to Donut Joe's, Rhonda's face lit up when she saw me.

With her gritty voice, she said, "If it isn't our local celebrity, Ms. Peaches Monroe!"

"Let me guess," I said. "You saw the photos."

"You looked fantastic," she said. "Breathtaking."

"You don't have to lie to me to get your dollar tip, Rhonda."

"I don't lie," she said. "I wish I looked as good as you, girl. And I'm excited about you dating the cute actor fellow. I thought there was a real spark between you two when you were here last week. So, what's it like?"

"Never boring," I said. "Give me one of these and one of these." I pointed to the two largest donuts. "Plus my mocha."

"Coming right up."

I looked around the cafe. There was only one other person in there. A petite girl. It was Josie Ranger, Dalton's half-sister. She had a baseball cap pulled down to her eyebrows. She could have passed as a teenaged boy, but she made eye contact with me for a split second, and I clocked her.

I said to Rhonda, "I've got time, so make my order to stay."

Rhonda handed me my mug and plate of donuts, which I took over to the table where Josie was sitting.

"You're not invisible," I said, taking a seat across from her. "What are you up to now? Trying to get a photo of me stuffing my face with donuts to sell to the highest bidder? What's the price on that sort of thing? I could always use a little extra for my savings account."

"It's not a lot," she muttered.

"Then you'd better start snapping and go for volume."

"It's perfectly legal," she said, not meeting my eyes. "If you're in a public place, it's fair game."

"How did you get the footage of us at the Weston Estate?"

She clamped her lips together.

I said, "I'll give you an exclusive of me eating this jelly donut if you tell me your secret."

She pulled out her camera. "Really?"

"Really. Tell me first."

"I put a tracker on Dalton's car. Then I contacted the Westons' security department and negotiated a deal."

"You've got a keen mind for business, Josie Ranger. Have you ever considered using your talents for good instead of evil?"

She slunk down in her seat. "This doesn't have anything to do with you. It's between me and Dalton. He's a bad man. He's going to break your heart, like he did mine."

"You two were dating?"

She bit her lower lip and nodded.

"That sounds awkward, considering you're brother and sister."

Her eyes flew open. "He told you about that?"

"Listen, Josie. I don't want to get involved in your family melodrama, but you pulled me in, so now you're going to get as good as you give."

She trembled in her chair. I was making my point.

I said, "Now take a picture of me eating this donut, then walk out the front door, and never come back to this street."

She nodded and raised the camera.

I ate the donut while pretending not to know she was there. I'd seen enough gossip websites to know what sort of unflattering food-hole-stuffing photos the general public liked seeing.

Josie Ranger took the photos and left without another word.

Rhonda came over a minute later and asked, "What was that all about?"

"I'm not entirely sure, but I believe it's over."

"Good. This is your fifteen minutes of fame, Peaches. You should be smiling and having fun."

"I love you, Rhonda, but you're nuts. Why would I be smiling about having half-naked pictures of me all over the internet?"

"Because people love you," Rhonda said. "It's all anyone's talking about today. I heard it on the radio before I even saw the pictures."

"Why would people love me?"

"Because you're a regular girl."

"You mean because I'm a fat girl."

"You're curvy," she said.

"So is a donut, but nobody wants to be shaped like one."

"There are some haters, of course, but most of the internet loves you. You made the top headline on the major sites. You squashed a bunch of politics news. You even squashed the news about the new superhero movie."

"I did?"

She nodded. "It's a good thing, Peaches. This is your moment. For the record, I'm totally Team Peaches."

"You're what?" Team Peaches was something only Nisha and I joked about. She was Team Peaches, and I was Team Nisha.

"It's a meme," Rhonda said, and she showed me.

There it was. Team Peaches. I was a meme. A positive one.

As surreal as it was to see myself as an object of admiration, it also made sense.

If I weren't me, but I saw a news story about someone like me skinny dipping with Dalton Deangelo then running through the woods in her underwear, looking as saucy and carefree as I looked, I'd admire that girl, too.

Chapter 30

The phone in the bookstore was ringing when I let myself inside.

I ran and answered, "Good morning, Bookworm Books."

A husky voice—Dalton's—replied, "Is this the real Peaches Monroe? The girl who's on everyone's mind this morning?"

"Guilty as charged. How are you doing? Did you get in trouble?"

"A little bit, actually." He sounded surprised. "How did you know?"

"You're famous and have a reputation to manage. People care about what you're doing. Me, I'm just a regular girl. I did get recognized at Donut Joe's this morning, but that's because Rhonda already knows me."

"You don't sound angry," he said. "I was worried you'd be upset with me."

"I should be."

"You weren't picking up your phone. I thought you were screening my calls. That's why I called the bookstore."

"Nisha confiscated my phone from me for my own protection. She thought it would be giving me bad energy all day because of the internet stuff. I've got a computer here at the store, but the internet access is restricted."

"Your best friend really cares about you."

"I'm a lucky girl."

"And I'm a lucky boy," he said. "I thought the trouble I got into from the studio would be nothing compared to the trouble I got from you."

I leaned against the counter, twirling the long phone cord around my hand. "Your sneaky little half-sister got most of my wrath already this morning. Did you know she put a tracker on your car? That's how she always knows where you are."

There was a pause, then Dalton said, "I'll have Bernard take care of the tracker after he pays you a visit."

"Bernard coming to see me? You'd better not be sending your butler to fetch me. I've got to work today. I may be a plus-sized internet sensation today, but these books aren't going to sell themselves."

"Bernard's coming over there with something for you to sign," Dalton said.

I snorted. "I'm not autographing any photos or memes."

"It's... something else," Dalton said. "When you get it, please don't be mad at me. My hands are tied. It's the studio, I swear."

"What is it? Some sort of restraining order where I have to stay two miles away from you at all times?"

"Nothing like that," he said warmly. "I would never stand for that."

"Good. Are you going to tell me what it is?"

"The first part is a basic NDA. A Non-Disclosure Agreement."

"Oh." I didn't know how I felt about that. It was a shock.

"Plus something else," he said. "A favor. You'd do me a favor, wouldn't you?"

"Is it a naked favor?"

He chuckled. "You're not far off." There was the muffled sound of someone telling him it was time to do something. "I have to go. Will you sign it for me?"

"Sure. For you, I'll sign it without even reading the fine print."

"Are you sure you're not mad at me?"

"It's your fault for making me go trespassing, but I accept full responsibility for looking so ravishing in my wet sports bra as I ran through the forest in terror."

"There's the spirit. Can you do me one more favor? Can you call me *babe*?"

"Sure, babe."

He sighed into his end of the call. "Off to work," he said.

I hung up the phone and got busy opening the store.

We had steady traffic that morning. Even though I got a few stares that seemed longer than usual, nobody asked for my autograph. Book buyers weren't as hooked on the day's internet news as some folks were.

After lunch, Dalton's butler arrived.

Bernard was carrying a briefcase and looking formal in his tweed suit and bushy mustache, as usual.

I was over at the table we used for unpacking new stock. A shipment had arrived. I was pricing and setting out new arrivals.

Bernard said stiffly, "I can come back later if this is a bad time for you, Ms. Monroe."

"Now is fine," I said. "The store will be quiet for a while." I pushed aside some paperbacks and slapped the table. "Throw that NDA down here, and I'll sign my life away."

Bernard frowned. "You should have your lawyer read it carefully."

"Why? I don't have a lawyer read any of those long software agreements I agree to almost daily. I'm sure some app is already the legal guardian of my soul."

His brown mustache condensed. Bernard continued frowning as he opened the briefcase and set a stack of papers on the table. The document was over a hundred pages long, I estimated.

I flipped to the first spot with a tab. "I heard you went for tennis lessons," I said.

"Yes. Thank you for the tip. I enjoyed the lessons at your local community center very much."

"Did you make any friends?"

He glanced away. "Not yet."

I started signing my name next to the yellow tabs that flagged signature pages.

"You ought to take the time to read the entire thing," he said. "I can come back later."

I waved a hand. "I'll just forget about it if you leave it here. I'd rather get it done now, thanks." I kept signing. There were a lot of signature spots. "Did your boss make you sign one of these yourself, Bernard?"

"Something similar," he said.

"How's the car? Your boss and I took it over some rough terrain."

"I know," he said flatly. "The suspension may never be the same."

"Blame your boss. It was all his idea."

"If I'd known what he had planned, I never would have taken the day off. I am truly sorry for what he dragged you into, Ms. Monroe. It would not have happened on my watch."

I finished signing the lengthy NDA and handed it back to him.

Bernard put it into his suitcase then handed me a large yellow envelope holding as much paper as what I'd just signed.

"Here's your copy," he said.

"I'll see that the smartest guy I know puts it somewhere appropriate," I said. "By which I mean my dad. He's got an office up the street, so I'll give it to him to keep in his filing cabinet."

"That's your business," Bernard said. "You should read it."

"Sure," I said. "Right after these." I pointed to a stack of new spy thrillers in our most popular series.

"The new one!" Bernard exclaimed. "But that's not due for release for another week."

"I know. These are going straight back into the box after I count them. Are you a fan?"

Bernard pouted. "Yes, but I can wait."

"You're going to have to," I said teasingly. "I'll set a copy aside for you. Come back next week."

"Thank you." Bernard started to fold up the briefcase but stopped. "I almost forgot the money." Bernard pulled a letter-sized envelope from the briefcase and handed it to me. "That's your signing bonus."

"My signing bonus?" I opened the envelope. There was a thick stack of cash inside. Enough to pay my share of rent at the house for a full year. "What's this?"

"That's your advance for the modeling job," Bernard said.

"What modeling job?"

He gave me an amused, told-you-so look. "You would know if you'd read the contract."

I picked up one of the spy thrillers. "Trade? You can have this now, but only if you tell me what's in the contract. A summary, not a five-hour spiel."

Bernard scrunched his mustache, eyed the spy thriller, then relaxed his mustache with a sigh.

He said in his usual formal tone, "In addition to the NDA, there was a contract for modeling a line of undergarments from a brand that's being promoted on *One Vamp to Love*. The designer saw your other modeling photos and loved your work. The corporate team was busy all morning in LA putting the deal together."

"That sounds fun and everything, but I'm not a model. Where did they get the idea I was?"

"They saw the photos of you at the hot spring, as well as the ones you did for a local yoga studio."

"They did?" He had to mean the pictures that Nisha's boss, Noah, must have already released for the studio's diversity campaign. "Holy porkchops. Who knew?"

"They must have liked what they saw." Bernard stuck his nose in the air. "I wouldn't know. I have not looked, and I will not look."

I clutched the stack of cash to my chest. "Did you say this was an *advance*? I may not be a lawyer, but I think that means there's more money coming. Am I right?"

He nodded. "Much more."

I squealed and hugged Bernard. He did not hug me back, but he did not run away screaming, either.

"Happy reading," I said, and handed him the spy thriller.

He wouldn't take it from me. He picked up the briefcase and backed away.

"I can wait," he said. "I'll get it next week."

"You're a good man, Bernard."

"Someone has to be." He nodded and left.

I hugged the cash to my chest and twirled.

I planned to call the smartest guy I knew to come over and help me read whatever it was I'd already agreed to, but then a customer walked in, and I forgot about the contents of the yellow envelope.

Chapter 31

Wednesday, May 18th

On my third day of internet fame, I was permitted to carry my own phone with me. Nisha had declared my energy to be very good, all things considered.

I hadn't seen Dalton since our outing as half-naked trespassers, due to his busy filming schedule. He had promised to try to swing by the house on Friday night for the party Nisha and I were throwing for a few old friends. It was unofficially a five-year high school reunion.

I had used some of my modeling advance moola to purchase party supplies, so we were proudly telling our friends to just show up. Food and booze would be provided. Just like at a real party for civilized adults.

Wednesday afternoon, my father strolled into the bookstore.

"It's chilly in here," he said. "You don't have the air conditioner running, do you? Open the front door and get some airflow for free."

"Did you stop by just to check on our power consumption?"

"I've got some epoxy curing back at the shop. Figured I'd save some brain cells by not sniffing it."

"Good choice," I said. "Oh, since you're here, take this." I handed him the envelope containing the NDA and the modeling contract I'd signed without reading it.

"Is it for your mother?"

"It's my modeling contract. Would you mind keeping it at your office? I'd stuff it in a drawer here, but Gordon Olivier might randomly show up and take a sudden interest in cleaning up the filing system."

He peered into the envelope. "Mind if I read it?"

"Someone should," I said. "I was planning to ask you to read it, but it seems like a moot point now."

He frowned. "I don't know anything about this whole modeling business."

"What's to know? It should be fun, and money is money."

I'd told him and Mom about the underwear modeling already—or at least as much as I knew so far.

The brand manager had been in contact with me by email to go over a shooting schedule. He had also made me promise not to lose a single pound before then. His name was Mitchell. We hadn't met, but I adored him already.

My father went over to the wall and adjusted the air conditioner settings. "Why wouldn't they get a professional model? You're a talented girl, but you've never done anything like this." He shook his head. "Everyone will see you. In your underwear."

"It's a bit late to put those horses back in the barn now," I said.

He gave me one of his no-nonsense fatherly looks. "It's never too late."

"Dad, do you not understand how the internet works?"

"Oh, I know how the internet works," he said. "I had an old college buddy call me out of the blue yesterday."

"That's nice."

"He called to let me know my daughter was on the internet, in scanty clothing."

"Get used to it," I said. "All your friends are going to be calling, and soon they'll be asking for my autograph. I'm basically a modern style icon now."

My father shook his head and adjusted the fan settings.

"I'm sorry your friend called you like that," I said. "I truly am sorry for the embarrassment I'm causing you and Mom, and Elliot."

"Elliot doesn't know yet. We'll deal with that when we have to."

"Good idea," I said. "He's only seven. Let him enjoy being a kid."

My father gave me a long stare, the look on his face softening by the second.

I nervously asked, "What?"

"Nothing," he said.

"What? Say it, Dad."

"Don't apologize," he said. "You're a beautiful girl, and I'm sure you'll look beautiful in those photos." He gave the fans one more adjustment. "This might be a great career move for you. I'm skeptical because I'm a parent and that's my job. But I'm also optimistic. I know you're a smart girl, and that you'll make the most of this."

"Thanks."

He took a deep breath. "Your mother and I are proud of you."

I ran out from behind the counter and hugged him.

He patted my back. "My little girl's growing up," he said.

"You're the best papa anyone could ever have. I can always count on you."

He cleared his throat. "Give me that contract of yours. I'll have a look through it."

I grabbed the envelope and brought it to him before walking him out.

He reached for the door but paused. "What's happening with the Stromquist boy?"

"Adrian? How should I know what he's up to? I haven't seen him since dinner last Friday. Why? Did you hear something?"

"I mean between the two of you. He's back in town for good, you know. His finances are in shambles for now, but he's young and hard working. He'll recover."

"Dad! We're just friends. That's all."

My father's eyes twinkled. "That's not what I heard. Your mother told me that Astrid told her that you two were caught kissing in the kitchen on Friday night."

"We were not," I said.

"All of the tea towels were soaked. I knew something must have been happening."

"None of it involved kissing, Dad. Someone in your gossip chain has been fabricating details."

"Are you sure?"

"My lips haven't touched Adrian's in almost eight years, and they're not going to."

"If you say so," he said, and then he left with the envelope.

Chapter 32

Nisha and I were relaxing in our spotless living room, enjoying a pre-party beverage before our friends arrived for our five-year high school reunion.

Nisha raised her glass to mine. "A toast to the new role model, Peaches Monroe. Cheers!"

"I'm no role model," I said with a snort. "Just because I'm full-figured and dating someone famous doesn't make me any better than anyone else. I didn't cure a disease."

Nisha winced. "Please don't say *full-figured*. Blimey! If you're full-figured, what does that make me? Half a woman?"

"Just on the bottom," I said. "Your hips could be wider, but your boobs are alright."

She playfully flicked me on the toe. "If you're going to be a positive role model for body acceptance, you have to embrace all the shapes."

"You know I do," I said.

"I know that, but I'm your best friend and I've known you forever. You have to watch what you say in interviews. For example, if you say your body is *real*, then does that mean other bodies are fake?"

"I'm not going to talk to anyone," I said. "I'll smile for the camera, then I'll disappear."

"There's no way you're going to disappear," Nisha said.

We both took a sip of our drinks. I didn't argue with her.

"So," Nisha said with a coy smile. "I kinda did something."

"Did you cast a spell on me? I found a wrinkled-up food-like thing at the bottom of my bed. Did you put one of your creepy talismans in there?"

"Of course not. You need to stop eating in your bed. It was probably just a baby carrot again."

"It had a face, Nisha."

"Do you want to hear my news or not?"

"Go ahead." I waved for her to speak then mimed zipping my lips shut.

"This morning, I went into Noah's office and finally let him have it. I told him that he's been taking advantage of me for years, and that he has to pay me more—a lot more—if he wants me to keep doing all the management work he should be doing."

I unzipped my lips so I could drop my jaw. "You did? You said all that?"

She nodded. "It was great. You should have seen me. It was like I was channeling you, Peaches."

"You make me so proud. How did he take it?"

"Oh, not well. He cried."

"Shut up."

"No. Really. He cried. He blubbered in my arms like a baby. He thanked me for *shining the light* on his flaws."

"And then he gave you a big raise?"

She shook her head. "And then he kissed me."

"Did you bloody well give him a double-punch to the butt?"

She looked away, the corner of her mouth turning up in a sly smile. "I went back to his house and slept with him."

I leaned back on the couch and crossed my arms. "This is not where I expected, much less wanted, this story to go. I'll have to double-punch him in the butt myself."

"After we were together, when I saw him lying naked in his bed, something happened. It was like all the artifice had been stripped away. All the artifice he shows the world, plus all the energy I've been projecting on him. I realized, in that moment, that he no longer had any power over me."

"The sex was that bad, huh?"

"So bad," she said. "So, so, so bad."

"You'd think a yoga studio owner would be better at sex."

"You'd think," she agreed.

"Then what?"

"Then I told him I quit. I walked out of his house, and I didn't even go back to the studio to pick up my things. I called the computer tech and told her to forward my email account to someone else."

"Your computer tech is a female?" I waved a hand. "Never mind. I'm getting off track. Good for you, Nisha. I'm happy for you. Do you think we're on our way to becoming actual grown-ups?"

Nisha bounced up and down on her chair. "I think so, Peaches."

"What are you going to do for a job?"

She stopped bouncing. "I haven't gotten that far yet."

The doorbell rang. Our first guests had arrived.

Chapter 33

Three Hours Later

The party was loud in the next room. Sunshine Banks had brought microphones, and people were singing karaoke in the living room. Everyone was having a good time, especially Nisha.

I was on my own, pulling some sausage rolls out of the oven for our guests, when Adrian Stromquist strolled into the kitchen.

"Here we are again," Adrian said. "Just me and you, alone in a kitchen on a Friday night."

"This is exactly how rumors get started," I said.

He grabbed a sausage roll straight from the cookie sheet. "Ouch! Hot! Hot!" He juggled the sizzling sausage roll from hand to hand. "Why is it so hot?"

"It just came out of the oven, genius."

He tossed the sausage roll high and caught it between his teeth. Then he breathed in and out heavily until it was cool enough to eat.

"Not bad," he said. "The samosas were better." He started going through the cupboards, found a platter, and started plating the sausage rolls. "Hot, hot, hot," he kept saying.

I handed him the tongs. "Use these."

"Good idea." He immediately pinched me on the bottom with the tongs.

I shook my head. "What's next? Soaking me with water and ruining all the tea towels?"

"You read my mind." He grinned and plated the sausage rolls using the tongs.

There was a knock at the back door. My father entered the kitchen without waiting for an invitation.

My father pointed at Adrian then me. "You two," he said with a knowing look and an eyebrow waggle.

"We're not kissing," I told him. "And we're not going to."

Adrian made a confused sound.

I explained to Adrian, "Your mother has been spreading rumors that you and I were kissing in my mother's kitchen last week."

My dad interjected, "It's my kitchen, too."

Adrian frowned. "I would remember something like that happening." He offered my father the plate of sausage rolls. "Careful, Mr. Monroe. They're nuclear hot."

My father shook his head. "I don't eat after nine o'clock." He handed me a thick yellow envelope. "I tried to read that contract you signed for the actor and his people, but I'm afraid I didn't get very far."

Adrian gave me a quizzical look and asked, "What contract?"

"None of your business," I said. "Take those sausage rolls out to the party guests, will you?"

"Where's the dipping sauce?"

"There's no dipping sauce," I said.

Adrian went to the fridge and grabbed the ketchup. "Here it is," he said. He got a small bowl from the cupboard, filled it with ketchup, nestled the bowl into the platter of sausage rolls, and looked at me expectantly.

"Perfect," I said. "You can cater all my future parties."

My father held his hands up, squirrel-like, and rubbed his fingers together. "Maybe just one," he said.

My father ate three sausage rolls dipped in ketchup. I took two sausage rolls to save for eating in a few minutes, then I sent Adrian out of the kitchen.

When the two of us were alone again, I asked my father, "What's wrong with the contract?"

"Mainly that it's a movie script," he said. "Not a contract."

I dug into the envelope and pulled out the thick document.

He said, "Sorry I didn't get to it sooner. Right after I saw you on Wednesday, we got a big shipment of the wrong parts from China. It was a whole thing."

"Don't worry about it." I looked over the document.

There was a movie title on the front page, and the rest of it was formatted like a script. I'd taken a screenwriting class in high school, so I was familiar with the formatting. I flipped to the back. The script was one hundred and twelve pages. Unlike Nisha, I did not read the last page.

"That's a script, all right," I said. "And it's not what the butler had me sign."

"Someone must have mixed up the documents," my father said. "Have the studio people email me a copy of the actual contract. I promise I'll read it right away." He gave me a sad look. "I'm sorry I let you down." There was a red smear on his cheek.

I handed him a napkin. "You'll be even more sorry if you get home and Mom sees ketchup on your face."

"Is there anything else I can do for you, sweetie?" He wiped his mouth.

A chorus of laughter floated in from the living room.

"Everything's under control here," I said.

"Is that Nisha singing? She sounds... is empowered the right word?"

"Nisha quit the yoga studio today, Dad. She finally told Noah to take his job and shove it."

My father's eyebrows went up. "Good for her. That man was taking advantage of Nisha's good nature. If she needs a work reference, tell her to let me know. I might even have some job leads."

I hugged him and thanked him for everything.

As he was leaving, he said, "As for you and the Stromquist boy, I hope I didn't walk in on anything."

"The night is young," I said. "There's still plenty of time for me to kiss Adrian, if that's what you're worried about."

"Really?" He gave me a hopeful look.

"No, Dad. Not really. My actual boyfriend, Dalton, is coming by later."

"He's your boyfriend now? It's official?"

"Yes. Maybe. I don't know. Do you want to stick around and ask him yourself?"

"I suppose I shouldn't. You kids will want to have your fun without me hanging around." He went to the door. "Petra?"

Butterflies fluttered in my stomach. My father only used my real name when he was deadly serious about something.

"Be careful," he said.

"You, too," I said. "Go straight home. No drive-through at McDonald's."

He gave me a stunned look. "How did you know?"

"You had ketchup," I said. "That's your trigger food."

"I could get one little cheeseburger," he said. "There's a new Jocko Ranger movie coming out, so I'll be hitting the gym anyway."

I patted him on the shoulder. "You do whatever it takes to have a wild and crazy Friday night. If you hit the drive-through, you'd better bring something home for Mom. That woman can smell ketchup on you from ten yards."

He nodded because it was true.

He left, and I was only in the kitchen long enough to eat my two sausage rolls and spill ketchup down the front of my shirt before Adrian came back in, his platter empty.

Adrian shook his head at my ketchup-stained shirt and used one of Nisha's English catchphrases. "Look at the state of you."

I held out my arms. "Adrian! Buddy! I don't believe we've hugged since you got back to town." I came at him, shimmying my chest and my big streak of ketchup.

"No, thanks, Ketchup Monster." He put his hand on my forehead and easily kept me at bay, thanks to his long arms.

I made zombie sounds and tried harder to get him.

He picked up the movie script with his free hand and looked it over. "Waterfall," he said. "What's this? A script?"

"Waterfall is just the working title," I said. "That doesn't mean they'll release the movie under that name. They'll probably do some test research."

"I know," Adrian said, using his know-it-all tone. "I took screenwriting with you, Peaches. Or do you not remember coming over to my house for our partner project?" He gave me a playful look. "I might have picked up a thing or two about screenwriting if you hadn't been all over me, demanding sex."

I stepped back. His hand dropped from my forehead, and his arm swung at his side.

"That's not how I remember it," I said. "I only wanted to work on our screenplay. It had real potential."

He flipped open the script. Without looking at me, he said, "You're the one who insisted we needed to do research."

"You're the one who kept writing more sex scenes into our screenplay."

"I had to do something," he said. "You kept putting in these long speeches where the characters talked about their feelings. That's not a good movie. A good movie has action." He flipped through the screenplay. "Like this one. There's a chase scene on page twenty. That's good."

I tried to get the script back. "Give me that. I'm not even supposed to have that."

He kept me at bay with one long arm again.

"Why wouldn't you have a copy? Isn't this your boyfriend's movie?" He turned his head so his eyes were in the shadows, appearing darker than usual. His upper lip curled, so that he looked vaguely menacing. "He is your boyfriend, isn't he? Dalton Deangelo?"

"Sort of."

"Now I understand what you said to me that night in the woods. He's renting an Airstream up there by the lake. I had a look at it last night. Not a bad setup."

"Now you're stalking Dalton?" I growled, "That's a new low, even for you."

He turned his face toward the light again. "Why so grumpy? Lighten up. We're having a party, Peaches. It's our five-year reunion."

"Give me back the script. He wouldn't want you reading it."

"Why not? Is it that bad?" He flipped to another page. "His character must be David. That's the name that's in here the most. Hey, I know. Why don't we do a script reading?"

"Adrian, stop being a jerk. I don't want to do a script reading with you."

"Come on. It'll be like old times. Isn't that what tonight's big reunion is all about?"

I glanced over at the door leading to the living room, where the party was carrying on without us.

"Fine," I said. "Just one page, then give it back to me."

Adrian grinned. "Let's do this. I'll be David. You be the girl, Harper."

"I don't even know what this movie is about."

"Let's read it and see." He went over to the oven and leaned against it, using the light from the range hood to illuminate the script.

I went over and stood beside him.

"Remember, I'm David," Adrian said.

I elbowed him to just get to it already.

Adrian said, in the deep voice he used to be more actory-ly, "'Those other guys didn't know a real woman when they had one. They're all such superficial phonies.'"

I read Harper's line. "'I know I'm not every guy's dream girl. I've got thunder thighs, and my chest kept hitting me in the face when we were running away from Old Man Carpenter's secret waterfall.'"

"'I know. Your chest hit me in the face, too.'" Adrian looked over at me. In his own voice, he said, "I think it's supposed to be a comedy."

"It's not very funny," I said as myself. "I don't want to do this, Adrian. It's a bad idea."

"What's the worst that's going to happen?"

The worst? I couldn't tell Adrian, but the worst was already happening.

Dalton had mentioned at least twice that he was doing research with me. He'd played it off as a joke, but now here was this script about him dating a chubby girl. A chubby girl he'd taken trespassing.

If I leafed through the pages, would there be a scene where he invited her over for dinner in his Airstream, then used his charm and good looks to get her into bed?

If I hadn't been so outraged over the prospect of having been used, I might have noticed my heart breaking into a million pieces.

How could I have been so gullible? I'd gobbled up Dalton's corny lines. He'd probably used everything from the script on me. And I'd fallen for it, just like chubby Harper.

Adrian was staring at me. He had no idea what was going on inside my head. He just wanted to keep reading the script so he could make fun of Dalton.

"We've read enough," I said flatly. "You've had your fun. Now let it go."

"You promised me one page," Adrian said, "Don't be sad, Peaches. I'm sure his next movie will be better."

"I'm not sad. Nisha's incense makes my eyes water." I grabbed a napkin and blew my nose.

"Let's see this thing through," Adrian said. "You need to know what you're dealing with. If you guys stick together, you can put those screenwriting classes to good use and help him pick better projects."

"That's not going to happen," I said.

"You never know," he said.

I waved for him to get back to the script already.

In his actor voice, Adrian said, "'Harper, forget about what shape or size we are. Let's just be two souls tonight. Two souls who are made of stardust and found their way back to each other, the way they were destined to.'"

My throat was on fire and my eyes were blurring, but I read my next line anyway. "'You're the one who left me here in this one-horse town, David. You wouldn't have had to find your way back if you hadn't left in the first place.'"

The next line read *David pulls Harper into a passionate embrace*.

Adrian said softly, "I'm not going to do that."

I lifted my chin and gritted my teeth as I smiled. "Why not? That's the problem with you, Adrian. You don't know how to fully commit."

"I'll show you fully committed." Adrian put his arms around me and pulled me in close. The ketchup on my shirt transferred to his, and he didn't notice. I was wearing shoes with heels, so his mouth wasn't nearly as far from mine as it had been the previous week.

In his actor voice, he gave me the next David line. "'Kiss me like I'm dangerous.'"

I died inside. Dalton had said that to me. I managed to spit out Harper's line, which felt like filler used for pacing because it didn't say much about her character. "'Up to your old tricks?'"

Adrian looked into my eyes, and he was no longer David. He was Adrian, the moody boy I'd pined for back in high school, but he was also a grown man, sexy and dangerous.

Adrian said the next line in his own voice, "'Kiss me like I'm bad for you.'"

I stared up at him.

He whispered, "Then they kiss. It says so in the script."

"I know," I whispered back.

"I'm fully committed," he said. "Is this what you want?"

"I..."

He leaned down, his lips getting closer to mine.

I could hear my pulse rushing in my ears.

I didn't realize the music in the other room had stopped. The party had been put on pause, thanks to the arrival of a certain celebrity. But I didn't realize that at the time, because all I was thinking about was the prospect of Adrian kissing me.

Adrian said, "You have to tell me what you want. It may be written in the script, but I won't kiss you if you don't want me to."

"I want you to—"

He kissed me.

I had been about to say, *I want you to, but I'm not thinking straight right now.* Or something like that. A *but* had definitely been planned.

He didn't hear the *but*.

That's why Adrian Stromquist was kissing me in the kitchen when Dalton Deangelo walked in.

The end of Peaches Monroe's Diary Book 1, Handful of Peaches.

To be continued in Book 2, Whole Lotta Peaches by Angie Pepper

www.ingramcontent.com/pod-product-compliance
Lightning Source LLC
Chambersburg PA
CBHW061304210726
48293CB00003B/1106

* 9 7 8 1 9 9 0 3 6 7 0 5 2 *